UNMOORED

ZARA HOFFMAN

ZH
press

UNMOORED

For Stefie

part one

If the bards of old the true has told
The sirens have raven hair.
But over the earth since art had birth,
They paint the angels fair.

L.M. MONTGOMERY

PROLOGUE

Ivy was sleeping when her door burst open. Her mother ran in, grabbed her by the arm, and pushed her into the closet. "Don't make a sound," her mother commanded before closing the door behind them. The sounds of booted footsteps started getting closer.

Through the gap in the closet doors, she could see the shadows of the intruders moving around her room as they searched for her.

"No one here!" one of them called.

"Check the closet," the other said.

Ivy moved further back behind the clothes and held her breath. The doors opened and she stood stock still. Moments passed before the doors shut again and she heard their retreating footsteps. But still, she stayed in the closet until hours later when her mother opened the door.

"We have to leave. Now." Her mother handed her a suitcase and told her to put on a large coat with a hood. "We're not safe here."

"Who were those men?"

"Hunters. Awful people. I'll tell you more when we're safe. But we need to leave now."

"What about everyone else?" Her grandmother, aunt, and cousin who had been visiting? Why weren't they with her mom?

"They're dead."

Ivy felt her heart drop. Who would want to murder her family?

"Where are we going?" she asked instead.

"To America. My friend promised to keep us safe."

"What was this?"

"I told you I'd tell you later," her mother snapped. "No more questions, Ivy. Now move."

"Ow! That hurt!" His sister glared at him as tears formed in her eyes. She held out her burned finger toward him in accusation.

Alec put the hot pan down and pulled his twin Fawn in for a hug. "I'm sorry." He didn't mention that he had told her it was hot.

She looked up at him with narrowed eyes. "You just don't want me to tell Mom. Why are you so mean to me?"

"That was an accident. I'm not *mean*. I'm your brother."

She blew flour at him. "Like that's better."

Stella reentered the kitchen and took in her messy children. "Go clean up, both of you. The rest of the family will be here soon." She walked over to the pan and looked at the two of them. "And in the future, use a mitt or dish towel before handling hot cookware."

Alec didn't say anything, but was certain his mom knew it was him. How she always seemed to know everything, he had no clue.

"Chop, chop," his mother said.

He and Fawn took off running toward their rooms. It was an unspoken rule that they were racing, and he was determined to win. This was going to be a fun Thanksgiving.

What they weren't expecting was their mom to call out, "Alec, Fawn, come meet my friend Leila and her daughter. They'll be staying with us until they get settled into their new home."

Alec saw the girl, who was only slightly taller than his shoulder, standing close to her mom and looking up at his own with uncertainty. He was going to say hi when his sister stepped forward and said, "Hi, I'm Fawn. Who are you?"

"I'm Ivy," she said. She looked at him before turning her attention back to Fawn. "Who's that?"

"That's my twin, Alec."

He walked over and waved before quickly stuffing his hand back into his jeans pocket. "Hi."

"Hi."

Stella and Leila looked down at the three of them and smiled. "Let's move things into the dining room, shall we? The rest of the family should be arriving shortly. Make yourselves at home."

Ivy followed her mother while he and Fawn stayed in the kitchen a little longer.

"How long do you think they'll be staying?" his sister whispered.

"I have no idea. But I like her a lot."

CHAPTER 1

8 YEARS LATER

"PEOPLE ARE GOING TO LOOK AT AND REACT to you differently. And not just boys your age. Girls and adults, too. No one in that school is immune to our charms."

Ivy suppressed the urge to roll her eyes. "I got it, Mom. This year will be different now that I finally have my siren powers. You've told me since we moved to America, my twelfth birthday would change how people react to me."

"Not just how others see you, but how you see others. Your tendency to sense relationships has always been there, but now it will be so much more powerful. You'll be able to *see* those connections now. That ability will help you find good prey when you need to feed."

Ivy made a face. She hated when her mother used that word. It made it sound like they were wild animals. It was dehumanizing and made her a little sick to her stomach.

They rolled to a stop and Leila looked over at her. "Oh, don't look like that. It's a natural part of being a siren. I've told you it doesn't hurt them."

"Do they feel anything?"

"They feel lighter, from what I've been told."

Ivy flipped down the passenger mirror and quickly examined herself. She had to admit she looked a little different. Even with the harsh lighting, she could tell her skin was clearer than it had been since turning twelve. It practically glowed. She closed the mirror. "And they have absolutely no idea why?"

"None, whatsoever. They assume it's a natural reaction." Her mother shook her head and turned on her blinker. "They can't even imagine another explanation."

Ivy unclipped her seatbelt and turned toward her mom. "Okay, but why? I don't feel any different than I did last year."

"Give it time, Ivy, but be careful who you befriend. Stay close to Fawn and Alec."

Her mom didn't directly mention it this year, but Ivy knew she was referring to the attack that had claimed members of their family only years before. It still terrified her when she remembered it. And thinking of her grandmother still brought her to tears. "I will." She kissed her mom on the cheek and opened the passenger door.

Fawn ran to her and gave her a tight hug. Alec continued at his normal pace and gave her a brief hug of his own before stepping back. "Did you cut your hair or something?" Fawn asked.

She shook her head.

"Something is different about you... Do you have a boyfriend?"

Ivy saw Alec tense beside his sister. "No. Definitely still single."

"I'll figure it out eventually. Come on. I don't want to be late." She ran up the stairs in front of them.

Ivy fought the urge to laugh. Their school was organized so counter-intuitively that it drove them all insane. Younger grades were at the top and the older they got, the less walking on stairs they had to do. "We have plenty of time. We're only on the fourth floor," she said, but Fawn didn't hear her.

"She doesn't care. She's the teacher's pet," Alec muttered.

"At least she won't flunk out like you," Ivy teased back.

"Hey, I'll have you know, staying as chill as me with such a Type A sister is a feat to be proud of."

"Sure, it is," she said, climbing the stairs with him.

B Y THE TIME LUNCH ROLLED AROUND, ALEC WAS ready to fight someone. Gym had just ended, and his idiot classmates decided to turn the locker room into a gossip hall. The topic of the day? How hot Ivy Moore had become. Which was ridiculous because Alec always knew she was attractive. Why was everyone so fixated on her appearance? She didn't even look that different. The girls in his other classes had been talking about her—some admiringly, most with barely concealed jealousy.

He grabbed his tray and took up residence in the corner of the student lounge, saving three seats with his feet, his jacket, and backpack. It was now part of the larger cafeteria but had once been its own room before the remodel had removed the connecting wall.

Dylan arrived first and moved his bag. "Thanks, man."

Fawn put on his jacket as she took her seat. He raised his eyebrow, but she shrugged. "It's cold in here."

Maybe it was, but he couldn't tell. In fact, his body felt so warm it might as well be the start of summer instead of mid-September.

Ivy was busy talking to the class jerk before she came over to them. She and Fawn insisted that he was a nice guy, but Alec had a weird feeling about him. Scott always seemed too polished. And if he *was* that perfect, maybe it was just his own jealousy speaking. But Alec didn't trust the guy. He watched Scott walk to the other side of the cafeteria and high-five his teammates in an uproar that was *almost* loud enough to drown out his own thoughts. He didn't know what made him do it, but he met Ivy's gaze and kept his feet on her chair.

"Real mature." She leaned down and moved his feet.

He ignored her, but he felt her gaze on him until Dylan started talking to her. Then it was his sister studying him. He pulled out his phone and began playing a game.

He heard Fawn say, "Are you coming over later?"

"I was going to," Ivy answered, "but something came up."

"You're going on a date?" The words were out before he could think better of it. And they sounded just as bitter as he suddenly felt.

"Just be careful," he muttered.

"He is right," his sister said.

He pushed back, put his bag on, and picked up his tray. "I'll see you at home later. Don't lose my jacket before then." He left before she could respond.

He dumped his food and went to the library. He pulled out a text-book but couldn't escape the one thought that kept going through his mind: *What* had *happened to Ivy? And why did he care so much?*

L ATER THAT NIGHT, IVY STOOD AT THE SUBWAY entrance. Scott looked at her, a cloud of light red surrounding him. She'd noticed it appear when he first saw her at school, and it had only become more distracting as their date went on.

"I had a fun time tonight," he said.

"I did, too." Which was a surprise since her mom had always told her to have very low, if any, expectations. Scott had taken her out to dinner and all they did was talk, contrary to his reputation. A common thread in all the stories was making out. And he hadn't tried once all night to even kiss her. Maybe her mom was wrong about her siren appeal. Maybe she was defective. She pushed that unpleasant thought down and smiled at Scott.

"Would you, maybe, like to go out again?" His gaze dropped down to her lips. She noticed the cloud around him become a darker and deeper color.

"Sure." She stayed still until his lips touched hers. Then she followed the instinct her mother had always talked about and kissed him back. His lips were a little chapped and he was adding a little too much and not enough pressure in turns, but it was okay. When he pulled back, she smiled at him again. "Well, I'll see you at school."

She descended into the subway. Once she grabbed a seat, which was surprisingly easier than usual, she pulled her latest romance novel up on her phone and settled in for the ride.

A LEC TOOK OUT HIS LAPTOP AND PULLED UP the history paper proposal he was writing. His teacher had already assigned the end of the year project and heavily emphasized that the earlier one started moving on it, the better the grade. And while he wasn't afraid of failing the class, he wanted to do as well as possible. As he'd gotten older, he lost interest in being on the school teams.

Or maybe he just didn't like the people anymore. The guys he'd known since kindergarten were starting to act like jerks, and he wasn't keen on spending any extra time with them outside of school hours. Dylan was the exception and the best friend he could ever ask for. His mom insisted he'd come home from the first day of kindergarten declaring he was his best friend.

Alec looked across the kitchen table at his sister. "You ready?"

She looked up from her own laptop and stopped typing. "Yep."

He shared the document with her. "Just tell me if it makes sense."

While he waited, he plugged in his headphones and went to his favorite online creator's website. He'd been so busy with homework during his free periods that he hadn't had time to watch the latest video when it had come out. The video was only halfway done when a text from his sister came through his computer. He paused the video, looked up, and took off his headphones.

"Finally. I've been calling your name for the past thirty seconds."

"You finished already?"

Fawn rolled her eyes. "You didn't write that much. And you know I read fast. Anyway, it's good. You have some grammatical errors, and I think you need to expand on, well, everything."

"It's a proposal."

"Ms. Thoroughgood will be more likely to approve it on the first go around if you flesh it out. *And* you'll have to do less work later."

"God, I hate it when you're right."

"Because it's most of the time?"

"Oh, shut up."

"Alec," his mom's voice sounded from the kitchen, "apologize to your sister."

"Sorry." How the hell did she hear so well? He used to assume it was a mom superpower when he was younger. Obviously, he now knew that was impossible. But he still hadn't figured out how his mom always seemed to know what he and Fawn were doing even when she wasn't with them. It was uncanny.

They both started typing again and didn't stop until Stella told them to put away their school work and help prepare dinner.

THE SUBWAY STOPPED. IVY WALKED QUICKLY UNTIL SHE stood in front of her best friend's apartment. She silently greeted the doorman who waved her past the desk immediately. Inside the elevator, she craned her neck back to stare up at the line of lit up numbers above the door as the metal box climbed the floors to the large penthouse.

Ivy was about to knock when Stella opened the door. "How was your date, Ivy?"

"Very nice." She hung up her coat in the closet and wandered into the foyer. "Is Fawn in her room?"

Her best friend's mom nodded. "Yes. Let me know if either of you need any snacks."

"Thank you," she called as she walked into her friend's bedroom. "Look at you: the perfect picture of a good student," she teased, seeing Fawn's desk already covered by books and notebooks.

Her friend looked up and smiled. "And look at you, fresh off her first date of the year. How was it? Tell me all about it."

Ivy laughed and pulled up the extra chair next to Fawn. "Well, nothing too exciting. We just talked, mostly. But he's nice. Not nearly the brainless jock we previously thought. He's actually smart. Well, at least when it comes to planning out his sports career."

"Really? He's already thinking that far ahead? Geez, I don't even know what I want to do for the rest of the year."

"I think he's just been expected to follow that dream since he was old enough to understand his father's words."

Fawn sighed. "Okay... Tell me what else you did. You didn't just talk, did you?"

Ivy touched her lips and smiled. "Well, he did kiss me goodnight."

Fawn leaned her elbows on the desk. "And how was it?"

"It was... okay." It had filled her with a new type of excitement she'd never felt before, but she had a feeling it had more to do with her siren powers. "He asked me out again."

"And what did you say?"

She smiled. "I said yes."

CHAPTER 2

Why couldn't he get Ivy's answer out of his head? He hadn't meant to eavesdrop on his sister's conversation with her best friend, but he'd been on his way to the kitchen and Fawn had left her door open. It wasn't like he was going to plug his ears in his own home.

"Alec?"

"What?" he asked, looking up at his sister.

She waved a hand in front of his face. "Are you back on Earth with the rest of us yet? What were you thinking about anyway?"

"Nothing." He glanced at the clock and was glad to see that homeroom was almost over. As he scanned the room, he noticed Megan Haskett watching him with undisguised interest. Their gazes met and she smiled before turning away quickly.

On his way to first class, he caught up with her. "Megan, how was your summer?"

"Good. What about yours?"

"Nothing too special."

She took a step closer, "Come on, I don't believe that."

He shrugged. "I really didn't do anything special." She was now in his personal space and he could smell her cherry-flavored shampoo. He swallowed, suddenly nervous. Before he knew what was coming, she pressed her lips to his. He closed his eyes and pressed his lips against her more eagerly. Her lips tasted like cherries.

He finally pulled back. Her eyes opened, and she smiled up at him. "Now I really don't believe your summer was boring if you can kiss like that."

"I'll tell you a secret, then. That was my first kiss."

She hit him in the chest.

He inhaled sharply. She was stronger than he expected. "What was that for?"

"You're lying."

"It's the truth!"

That seemed to flip a switch on in her because she slammed her lips against his again. He lost awareness of how long they kissed this second time, but when he felt someone watching them, he pulled away.

Ivy stood in the hallway, her arms crossed over her chest and a pissed expression on her pretty features.

IVY COULDN'T BELIEVE WHAT SHE WAS SEEING, AND she would have *loved* to ask Stella to cast a forgetting spell, but then she'd have to explain why and she didn't have an answer for that simple question. And clawing her own eyes out sounded too painful.

When she'd gotten the strange energized feeling that seemed to come with being a siren, she'd made an excuse to go to the bathroom and investigate what the source was. Now she sincerely wished she hadn't. Curiosity did kill the cat, after all.

And then it got worse because the girl kissing Alec was none other than Megan Haskett, resident queen bee and mean girl. The devil-incarnate turned to her and sent her a smug smile before kissing Alec one more time. She said, "See you later, Alec," loudly enough for Ivy to hear then walked down the hall toward her class.

"I can't believe you just did that."

He walked closer and she fought the urge to scan his appearance again. Why did he have to be so good looking? "Are you jealous, Ivy?"

"Do you know who that is?" She didn't wait for him to answer. Of course, he did. But she still clarified. "In case you forgot, that's the girl who regularly bullies your sister. Just thought you should keep that in mind the next time you decide to lock lips with her. And in case you decide to continue this stupidity, don't do it in front of Fawn. I mean it. I don't want to have to clean up your mess because you were too focused on kissing instead of your twin's feelings."

Not giving him a chance to answer, she turned on her heel and walked quickly back to class. Her bathroom break was long enough to make even the laid-back Mr. Ashwell raise his eyebrows when she reentered his class. She slid into her seat so fast she almost fell right off on the other side. Luckily, he continued his lecture without comment.

Fawn leaned over to her once Mr. Ashwell turned his back and whispered, "What took you so long?"

Ivy shrugged. "There was a line," she answered softly.

She gave her an incredulous look but didn't call her on the ridiculous excuse. Just another reason Fawn was her best friend.

A LEC WAS ANNOYED. HE'D BEEN SOMEWHAT HAPPY FOR the few moments while he was kissing Megan, able to forget the fact that Ivy was going on another date with Scott, but that didn't last long. And then, of course, Ivy further sank his mood by criticizing his choice.

He'd heard Fawn complain about her enough times to know about Megan being a bully. Ivy's suggestion that he would actually get involved with his sister's tormentor pissed him off. It wasn't as if *he* had initiated the kiss.

Unfortunately, thinking about Megan seemed to conjure her because she headed straight for his table. Across from him, he saw Fawn shrink in her seat and Ivy send him a death glare. Dylan muttered, "Look out. Something wicked this way comes."

Ivy snickered, but he refused to look at her.

"Oh, how sweet," Megan crooned. "You're sitting with your little sister and her one friend. Excuse me," she said to Dylan who was quick to move over. "I missed you during class," she said too sweetly, leaning over the table.

When she leaned in for a kiss, he turned away. She looked at him like he'd lost his mind and he kind of felt like he had, too. Ivy had been right. Kissing Megan had been an idiotic thing to do. "I'm sorry, I never said that we'd kiss again. And after you just insulted my sister right in front of me, it's *definitely* never happening." When she didn't immediately go, he added, "That's your cue to leave."

"You jerk!" She turned on her heel and ran out of the cafeteria.

When the doors closed behind her, people started talking all at once. He hadn't even noticed that they'd ever stopped. Dylan turned to him and said, "I know she's had a crush on you for a few years, but I still can't believe it. You *kissed* that reptile?"

He refused to meet Fawn or Ivy's gazes but nodded. "She caught me off guard after homeroom."

Dylan whistled. "Well, you certainly took her down a peg."

"Alec." He looked up at his sister. She didn't look angry. He blew out a silent breath of relief. "Thank you for that."

Ivy rolled her eyes. He knew she was probably thinking it was his fault to begin with.

Scott and some of his friends came over to their group. Alec curled his hand into a fist under the table when he saw Scott and Ivy share a smile. He was surprised when his classmate then addressed him and said, "Well, Belgrave, who would have thought you had it in you to go up against the Ice Princess and win?"

Alec shrugged and didn't say anything, knowing that if he did, he'd probably start another fight. But this one would result in more than just hurt feelings.

"Anyway," Scott continued. "Just wanted to congratulate you on giving her a taste of her own medicine. She definitely deserved it. You're pretty cool, Belgrave."

"I guess we should call you 'lady killer,' huh?" one of the others said.

"Does it look like we're in an 80's movie?" another griped.

Scott turned his attention back to Ivy. "We still on for tomorrow night? You can pick the movie."

Out of the corner of his eye, Alec saw Ivy lean forward and smile. "Absolutely. I can't wait."

"See you around, Belgrave." With that, Scott and his group went back to their table. He noticed some of his female classmates were watching him with fascination.

He met one girl's gaze and she blushed before turning and whispering to her friend.

He turned back around and saw Ivy looking annoyed. "What's the matter? Not looking forward to that date anymore?"

She scoffed. "You wish."

"Not really." He forced his voice to stay steady and aloof. "Who you date isn't my concern. He obviously isn't a bad guy if you said yes to a second date." Yeah, right. *Just keep telling yourself that.*

His response seemed to surprise her. A pause passed before she said with a little more volume than necessary, "Exactly."

Silence descended on their table. "So..." Dylan started, turning to Fawn. "Can we just agree that Mr. Ashwell got even cooler since this summer. What do you think it is?"

Fawn laughed. "That story about when he saw Laurence Olivier perform on stage? Who in their right mind insults Laurence freaking *Olivier's* acting talent?"

Alec saw Ivy nodding along but could tell she didn't know what they were talking about. "When did he tell this story?" he asked.

"Oh, this morning during first period," Dylan said, glancing over at him before turning back towards his sister.

"You had just left," Fawn clarified.

"I'm sure he'll tell it again in a week or so," Ivy said.

"Do you want to do the reading together after school today?" Dylan asked, drawing Fawn's attention back to him.

"Sure. Meet you in the library after last class?"

He smiled. "Yes."

Ivy sent Dylan a knowing smile and Alec sent her a look that he hoped said, *What the hell?* She shrugged and grabbed her bag. "Well, see you."

"Bye, Ivy," Fawn said.

Dylan glanced at him, then the clock and said, "I'm going to go, too. See you around, Fawn, Alec."

That was so sweet of him! Standing up for his sister like that." Ivy rolled her eyes at the sighs that followed that announcement.

Sweet of him to kiss his sister's bully. If they wanted to create a false image of Alec Belgrave, who was she to burst their bubble by telling them he was as clueless as every other guy in school?

Between their fawning and the number of guys she'd heard talking about Alec brushing off Megan, she was ready to punch something.

Preferably someone. Specifically, Alec. But she wouldn't. Ivy looked over at the group of guys talking so loudly they might as well have been holding microphones hooked up to the school's speaker system. Whatever sexist said that guys didn't gossip was an idiot and probably deep in denial.

Fawn walked over and let out a frustrated sigh.

"Did Megan say something to you? I'd be happy to kick her ass."

Her friend smiled. "Thanks, but that's not it. Though I may take you up on that offer the next time she says something. Which will probably be soon now that my brother humiliated her."

"Okay, so what's the problem?"

"I'm going to sound so ridiculous." Fawn pulled her friend into the bathroom and checked underneath each stall for feet to make sure it was empty except for them.

"Calm down, Jane Bond. No one is listening in. We're not interesting enough for anyone to care that much about us."

"Ha," her friend deadpanned. "Okay. I'm just... I'm upset that both you and my brother have kissed someone, and I never have." Her words came out in a rush as if slowing down would cause her to lose her nerve. "And I'm sure Dylan has, too, which means I'm the odd girl out."

Ivy smiled at her. "It's not that big a deal, Fawn. And honestly, as Alec just proved, kissing just anyone isn't a good idea."

Fawn fixed her with a probing gaze. "You never did tell me where you were this morning."

"I caught them kissing. That's why I was gone longer than usual."

Her friend made a gagging sound. "I don't want to hear about it. I still can't really believe he did that to begin with."

"Same here."

"But I still wish I wasn't the only one out of us who hasn't been kissed yet."

Ivy sighed. "I'm positive Dylan has a crush on you." She saw a cloud of pink around him, reaching out to Fawn as he asked her to study with him. She'd never seen anything like it before, but she knew instinctively what it was and that it was a product of her newly amplified powers.

"Really? Wait, so is studying together a date in his mind?"

Ivy shrugged. "I don't know. I'm not a mind-reader."

"That would be so cool."

"I wouldn't want to hear if people were thinking mean things."

"I guess that's true. Anyway, thanks for dealing with my craziness. Sometimes I just wish guys looked at me like they look at you. Especially this year."

"Don't worry about it, Fawn. It'll happen when it's supposed to."

DYLAN SLID INTO THE SEAT ACROSS FROM ALEC and cleared his throat. "Can we talk?" They sat at one of the smaller tables in the back of the library.

"Sure. But first, please tell me why I can't balance this stoichiometry equation." He pushed his sheet of paper across the library table. "I feel like my brain is about to explode. I have chemistry right after this free period."

Dylan looked at the sheet for a few minutes then said, "your mole conversion is wrong." Then he wrote out the correct formula in the margin and handed him back the sheet. "Anyway, what I wanted to tell you is... don't get mad... I like Fawn."

"That's good since she's my sister." He realized what his friend was getting at. "You're my best friend so I know you're a good guy."

Dylan let out a huge breath and Alec felt bad about how nervous his friend had been.

"Am I really that intimidating?"

"Well... she's your sister. And to be honest, you can get a little aggressive when protecting her. Which is great when it's against the many jerks of our grade, but it made me nervous."

Alec couldn't help but feel slightly amused at his friend's anxiety.

Dylan must have noticed because he said, "It's not funny."

"It is just a little. I mean, come on, you could easily take me down. I'm not much of an obstacle."

"As if I'd ever actually fight you." His friend looked at him for a little too long.

Alec cleared his throat. "Was there something else you wanted to talk about?"

"What's going on with you lately? You've been in a pissy mood."

"It's nothing."

"Want to try saying that again? Because I definitely don't buy that pathetic lie. And I know you don't either."

"Girls are just driving me nuts lately. Between Megan and all the attention I got this afternoon, I feel like I'm drowning."

"Girls in general or one in particular?"

Alec put the sheet into his backpack and stood up. "I gotta go or I'll be late. Thanks for the help."

"No problem. Good luck with the girl trouble. And good luck in chemistry. See you around."

CHAPTER 3

"ANY BOYS THAT HAVE CAUGHT YOUR EYE?" HER mom asked. "What about Scott? You said you were seeing him for another date? Hand me the large strainer, please."

Ivy continued to chop the onions, hoping she could go fast enough to avoid needing a break. "Yeah. But I don't have strong feelings about him. He's nice, but there's not much of a connection." She felt her eyes start to sting and wiped them with the back of her hand. God, she hated cutting onions almost as much as she loved eating cooked ones. It wasn't fair.

Leila made a small sound of sympathy. Or was it empathy? "That's okay, Ivy. You won't bond deeply with everyone who shows interest in you. It's statistically impossible. As sirens, that number is multiplied, so the chance of that are even lower for us. That doesn't mean that you can't have fun. As long as you're being safe and smart about it."

Her tone became more serious at the end and Ivy turned to face her mom. "I'm being safe, but it's not going to happen with him."

"I'm not saying it will. But you should always be prepared."

Ivy suppressed the urge to emphasize that she wasn't heading down that road, but realized it was useless. "I will be," she conceded.

"Throw that into pan when you're done."

Ivy made a final cut and then put it in the simmering oil. Her mother added chicken and Ivy worked up the nerve to ask one of the questions that had been plaguing her since school started. "I don't feel like my powers are always working."

Leila cut and dropped another piece of chicken into the pan. "You told me that some people at school and even strangers were reacting to you more favorably."

Ivy poured out the bag of parsley into the colander and rinsed the leaves. Then she dried them with a paper towel and placed them on the cutting board. "Well, yes... but I thought you told me that being a siren would make people attracted to me. When I went on my date with Scott, I think he was into me the whole time, but he didn't kiss me until we said goodnight."

"If you weren't interested in him, you might have been dampening your effect on him. You'll learn eventually how to avoid that so you'll be able to feed from anyone."

Ivy began cutting the parsley with a little more force than necessary, practically smearing green on the white surface with each drag of the knife. "But why would I want to?"

"I've told you before, Ivy. When you get older, you'll need to feed more. And to do that, it's best to be less picky and have multiple sources at a time. You don't even have to be involved with them. Eventually, you'll be able to feed off strangers."

She wasn't looking forward to that part of being a siren. "But nothing is wrong with me?"

"Of course not. You're perfect the way you are."

A LEC WINCED WHEN HIS KNUCKLES HIT THE BAG. He looked down at his hand and flexed. That was going to be sore tomorrow.

"Here." Alec turned to see Marcus, Dylan's dad, standing beside him.

"You need to hit like this." He demonstrated a hit, then pointed to the flat part between his knuckles on his fist. "You want this area to make the most contact. If you do it the way you were doing, your knuckles will take the biggest beating and make it harder to continue."

"Thanks." He threw another punch and found not only did it hurt less, but the bag moved more.

He looked over at Dylan who was working on one of the machines before moving to the other side of his bag so he could also watch the two boxers in the ring under Marcus' careful instruction. To say they were ripped would be an understatement. They looked like they belonged next to his sister's magazines of Hollywood action stars.

Alec continued punching. He wasn't unfit, but watching the other guys, even Dylan, transform, made him feel a little inadequate.

"When they're done, we can take a turn," his best friend said. "You up for it?"

"You're on."

After twenty minutes of getting his ass handed to him, Alec said, "I'm done," and climbed out of the ring. It wasn't to say that he hadn't landed anything on Dylan, but his own body had taken the maximum it could handle.

He grabbed his bottle from the side and drank a large gulp of water. Next to him, Dylan plopped down on the bench and poured water on his head from his own water bottle. Then he shook his head, spraying Alec in the process.

"Hey! Warn me next time I'm in the splash zone. That's not what I agreed to when you asked me to box with you and your dad."

"Sorry, dude. I just needed to cool down. My skin feels like it's on fire lately."

"Do you have a fever?"

His best friend shrugged. "Nope. Dad says it's normal."

Normal for what? Alec glanced at Marcus who was busy wiping down their gear. "Well, if he says it is, I'm sure your fine."

"You seemed kind of angry during sparring. You okay? Still having girl problems?" His friend smirked, and Alec suppressed the urge to punch him in the arm. Hard.

"I've got it under control."

"If it's anything like your right hook, it needs work."

"Well, at least it's not worse than your roundhouse kick. That was just sad."

"Oh, shut up."

"Come on, let's go get something to eat. I'm starving. Thanks, Marcus!" he called out.

"You're welcome, kid! Don't forget to ice when you get home. Your mom would kill me if you got seriously injured under my watch."

"I will." He turned to Dylan. "I still can't believe your dad owns a boxing studio."

"It's been years, dude. When will that ever not impress you?"

"Probably never."

"I want a hotdog. What about you?"

"Sounds good to me."

So..." Ivy looked up and saw her classmate Andrew leaning on her lab table. Fawn had turned around and was talking to Dylan and her brother at the table behind them. "I hear you're going out with Scott. How's that going?" He had a knowing expression on his face that she didn't like.

"Fine?" Why the hell was he asking? "We went on one date and have another one coming up."

"Well, if you get bored with him, I'm here."

"I'll keep that in mind," she replied. *Just as soon as Hell freezes over*, she silently added. There was no way she would ever go out with someone who had such little integrity that they tried to steal their friend's date behind their back. She had standards, after all.

He went back to his seat and Ivy flipped to a new page and continued copying the stoichiometric equation from the board. *Why* they were spending a whole week on it was beyond her. In her humble opinion, it was a cruel and unusual punishment.

Fawn, who had obviously been half-listening asked, "Isn't he Scott's best friend? What's he doing asking you out behind his back?"

"I don't know." But she had an idea. And she didn't like the likely conclusion that her siren powers were bringing out the worst in people. Like the world needed anymore of that.

Fawn turned her paper and Ivy saw that she had solved one of the parts that was stumping her. "Seriously, what is up with you? Guys are practically falling over themselves to talk to you. What's your secret? I need all the help I can get."

"Dylan still hasn't asked you out?"

Fawn shook her head. "Should I ask him?"

Ivy looked over her shoulder at Dylan. He was watching her best friend and practically stewing in a cloud of pink. She caught his gaze and surreptitiously eyed Fawn. He silently mouthed back, "I'm working on it."

She glanced at Alec, and Dylan nodded. Ivy turned back to her best friend. "I would give him a little more time. Maybe he's just shy."

"Dylan is anything but shy."

Ivy shrugged. "Attraction makes people do stupid things. At least, that's what my mom says."

Fawn blew out a breath, sending her pencil rolling toward the end of the table. She caught it before it fell. "Well, that's not comforting at all."

"You know my mom isn't one to sugar coat things. She's not like your mom."

"Yeah, I do. But your mom is awesome in her own way."

"True."

"Okay," Dr. Valenstein said, bringing their focus back to the matter at hand. "Who wants to come up and share their solution for the first equation?" He held out the smart marker as an invitation to them all. There was absolutely *no* way she was going up there. Fawn raised her hand and went up to the interactive board.

While her friend was up there, Ivy quickly ripped out a page in her notebook and wrote down, *Stop wasting time and ask her already.* With Fawn almost done with the equation, she shoved the note under Dylan's notebook.

She heard him open it. Maybe he would finally get the message and ask Fawn out. Because as much as Ivy was all for supporting her best friend, she was sick of Fawn's misery being prolonged because he hadn't yet gotten up the nerve to tell her how he felt.

Alec turned to his friend. He'd seen him and Ivy's semi-private exchange. "I take it she knows about your crush on my sister?"

Dylan nodded. "She guessed on her own."

Of course, she had. "You know, I think you're supposed to tell the person you like that you like them *first.*"

Dylan looked back down at his paper and began studiously copying the writing Fawn was doing from the board. "Shut up, man."

"Why? Someone has to hold you to it. When are you going to grow a backbone and ask my sister out? It's not like she has cooties."

"Of course, I know that. We're not in kindergarten anymore. And me wanting to wait doesn't mean I don't have a backbone, asshole." Dylan put down his pencil and looked at him. "What is it with you and Ivy bugging me about this? Maybe I want to move at my own pace."

"You can't blame us. My sister is getting boy fever, and neither of us want to hear much more of it."

Dylan rolled his eyes. "I'm not going to start my romantic relationship with your sister as a favor to you. We may be best friends, but even I won't do that."

"That makes you the right guy for her. But, seriously, hurry up."

At the end of class, Alec wrapped his arm around Fawn's shoulders. His sister shrugged him off and looked at him as if he had grown a second head. "What's up with you?"

"Nothing. Can't a brother be affectionate with his sister?"

"Not when that person is *you.*"

He rolled his eyes. "Fair enough. So, want to help me out with the rest of the lab? I couldn't get the end part."

"Alec, he did those right on the board. Weren't you paying attention at all during the end?"

No, not really. He'd been too busy observing Ivy.

"Seriously, what is up with you lately?"

He didn't answer and she didn't push the issue. "Will you help me or not, Fawn?"

She nodded. "Of course, I will. But you'll owe me."

"I can live with that."

CHAPTER 4

Ivy saw two familiar silhouettes standing in the concessions line. Ivy waved until her best friend saw her. "Fawn?" Dylan was standing beside Fawn and they both came over. She sent Fawn a look that said, *You're on a date?*

Her friend sent back a look that barely contained her excitement. "Hey, you didn't tell me you were coming here tonight. Hi, Scott."

"Hey," Scott said, barely paying Fawn any mind.

"What movie are you here for?" Dylan asked.

"The new horror film," Ivy answered. "What about you?"

Her friend looked at Dylan and held onto his arm tighter. "Same."

"Really?" She looked at Dylan who had the grace to look slightly embarrassed. He may be a good guy, but it was clear what his plan was.

"Well, you know I want to become less scared of things, so I figured I should start now."

"Uh huh. Well, I guess we'll see you in there."

She turned, ready to go inside the auditorium when she saw Alec enter with a date. She didn't recognize the girl.

Her hope that he wouldn't notice her went right out the window when Dylan called out, "Hey, Alec! Over here."

And, of course, he and his date came right over.

He smiled at Fawn and Dylan, but then his smile almost became a grimace when he saw Ivy and her date. "Ivy, you're here."

She nodded, unsure of what to say. As she looked at them, she didn't need special powers to see that that the girl cared about Alec a lot more than he appeared to care for her. It was clear in the body language, but having her siren abilities confirm what she suspected helped temper the irrationally hurt feeling she felt seeing Alec with someone else. The girl was practically smothered in a pink cloud.

Scott threw his arm around her and she fought the urge to move away from him. "Let's go in."

Once inside, Ivy saw Alec and his date beeline for the front while Fawn and Dylan found a spot somewhere in the middle. She led Scott toward the back of the theater. As she sat down, he looked back and frowned when he saw her. He quickly turned around and sat back down.

Like her, he was sitting on an aisle. In the past when the three of them went to the theater, they had always argued about which one of them got the seat until Stella either took it herself or gave it to Fawn, who didn't care about where she sat as long as she could see. Seeing Alec lean in to kiss his date made Ivy wonder if aisle seats weren't as amazing as she always thought.

When the lights went down, she was glad to finally focus on something other than Alec's dating life. It wasn't her business, so she shouldn't care. Too bad telling herself that didn't seem to make it any easier for her to witness. And then there was the energy in the air that made her feel like she'd one too many sugar-filled specialty drinks at her favorite coffee shop. Whoever said caffeine was the best, clearly underestimated sugar. It was something she'd never felt before her birthday, and only a few times since. Yesterday was the first time she'd felt it since her American cousins had been staying over with their dates for the weekend. She wished she didn't know what the sensation meant, but it was undeniable. Unlike her favorite Queens-based superhero, her extra sense didn't alert her to danger. It made her hungry in a way that no food or drink could satisfy.

She saw her date who was watching the coming attractions as they flashed across the screen. "Scott," she whispered.

He turned to look at her. "Yes?" His voice was rougher than usual.

Desperate to release some of the energy building inside her, she leaned in and kissed him. He groaned and placed his hands on her hips. She felt their heat as if he were branding her, which only made her more eager. She licked and sucked on his lips until he opened up, but he was the one who plunged his tongue into her mouth.

They continued to make out until she felt his hand drifting lower and lower. When he tried to sneak his hand under her skirt, she pulled back and grabbed his wrist, halting his progress.

He stared at her looking almost as hungry as she felt.

"I didn't say you could touch me."

He grinned. "That sounds like an invitation."

"It's not."

He leaned in. "Come on, Ivy. We were having fun just then. No need to stop now."

He started to pull her back in, but she put a hand on his chest. "Scott, stop."

His lustful expression turning into one of anger. "You're such a tease." He grabbed his coat and brushed past her, leaving the auditorium. The door slammed shut beside her.

Ivy stared at the screen, her body going cold all of a sudden. She could still feel the remnants of the siren rush, but she had no desire to feed that hunger anymore tonight. She saw Alec was still busy with his date and couldn't stop a tear from falling. She wiped it away, gathered her belongings and quietly left the movie.

ALEC HONESTLY COULDN'T SAY WHAT THE MOVIE HAD been about when the theater lights came on. He'd been so focused on distracting himself with Aimee that he might as well have saved the thirty dollars he'd spent on the tickets and concessions.

Aimee started to stand, but he still sat, absently watching the credits roll. A habit ingrained by his mom. He looked over and saw his sister and Dylan still there. He hadn't expected to see them at the theater, much less Ivy and Scott. He turned to check in on them. Even with all the people emptying out of the theater, he could see that they had vacated their seats.

He felt a pressure on his head as he was overwhelmed with an inexplicable rage. Which was absolutely ridiculous. Ivy was her own person who could make her own decisions. Even if it was to go out with one of the biggest jerks in the grade and take things farther than she should. She was like a sister to him. He was only concerned with her safety.

Liar. Alec forced himself to take a deep breath and slowly let it out. His mom was always going on about meditation, but it had never helped him before. But desperate times called for desperate measure. Okay, so maybe his anger wasn't all about protecting Ivy as he would Fawn. Seeing her kiss Scott during the film previews had been a special kind of torture.

When it was only him, Aimee, Fawn, and Dylan, he stood up and they walked out as a group. Aimee looked at her phone and said, "Well, it's late. But thank you for a really nice night. I hope we can do it again some time."

"I'll call you," he said. Even as he said the words, he knew he wouldn't. It wasn't that there was anything wrong with her, but he felt no spark between them.

She left, leaving him with his sister and Dylan.

"I'll say goodnight, too," his friend said, "I had a fun time, Fawn."

She smiled at him so brightly, even Alec felt his mood lift. "Me, too, Dylan." She paused. "Would you like to go out again?"

"I'd love it." He kissed her on the cheek then glanced at Alec. "Well, I'll see you both tomorrow."

When he was out of earshot, Fawn said, "Before you ask, we didn't do anything but watch the movie. Unlike you and Aimee. How come I've never heard of her? You seem to like her a lot."

He shrugged. "I don't think I'll see her again."

"Well, you might want to work on not sending mixed messages in the future because I bet with the kisses you gave her, she's expecting at least a second date."

"If you were watching me so closely, like you claim, how were you watching the movie?"

She pushed him, but not enough to make him lose balance.

"Nice try," he said.

She huffed. "You know what I meant."

They walked in silence into the subway. When they were seated, she said softly, "I really like Dylan."

"I'm happy for you."

"Really?"

"Well, yeah. You're my little sister and he's my best friend. I want you to both be happy, and if that's with each other, that's cool."

"I'm your *twin* sister."

He smiled. Of course, that's what she cared about.

When they got home, they told their mom about their dates and then retreated to their rooms. "Goodnight!" Fawn called from hers.

Alec sat down at his desk and pulled out his homework for the week. As much as he knew it would be better to go to sleep, he also knew that if he didn't tire himself out productively, he'd be focusing on what Ivy might be doing. And that would keep him up all night. So, homework was the better alternative.

He opened the school-given copy of *Macbeth* and frowned. He'd read it twice already, as had his sister. Their grandmother had gifted them a Shakespeare omnibus a few years back, and they'd taken turns reading each of the plays. But his current English teacher was driving him nuts. Who could conceive of someone ruining such a master-piece of literature? As if that wasn't enough, the homework was to underline words he "didn't understand" and to write his guesses of their meanings in the margin based on the rest of the sentences.

If it wasn't his favorite play, he'd have thrown it. His grandmother had taught him and Fawn the importance of grammar, being able to type without looking at the keyboard, and the dictionary. There were no words in it that he didn't know the meaning of. And what's worse, the teacher was crazy enough to do book checks. He rolled his eyes. God, save him from crazy English teachers. And to think it was Fawn's favorite subject. He shuddered. People who assumed twins were ex-act copies were wrong. He clicked his pen and took a deep breath. What words could he pick without looking stupid? None.

Alec began circling and annotating his thoughts on the book from memory. Then, he opened his laptop and began outlining the themes of the novel: fate, free-will, ambition, and violence. He could write an essay about each of them. Not that he would. He started grouping them by changing the font color and began an outline about how it was Macbeth's perceived lack of free-will that set his fate in stone.

His teacher loved irony, and that premise was filled to the brim with it. He checked the clock and noticed that it was barely midnight, and yet he was still too wound up to go to sleep. Alec opened yet another document and began free-writing the introduction and first paragraph of his paper. He knew that it was probably garbage, but he had to do *something* to block out his frustrating, errant thoughts.

By the time he was done with that and everything else, he was almost falling asleep where he sat. He pushed back and turned off his light. He felt his way to his bed and fell into a dreamless sleep.

CHAPTER 5

"How's being a siren treating you? Find any new admirers?" Clearly, her mom hadn't told her cousin Grace about Scott. And she thanked God for that.

"Well, it's a lot more overwhelming than I thought it would be, but okay, I guess." She started moving toward the kitchen again. This was definitely not a talk she was ready to have.

"It'll get better with time, dear. But you should know that if you don't learn to focus on the individual, you'll always be overwhelmed. A siren out of control is not a good thing. Don't let it happen to you. Hold on there, tiger," she added, "Come here, take a break and sit."

As much as Ivy loved her family, there were a few members that she preferred not to be stuck with in a conversation alone. It wasn't that Grace was mean or even passive aggressive, but her level of nosiness made even *Ivy* look tame.

Grace's daughter, Gemma, also came over. "Mom, let's not grill Ivy, okay? It's only been a few days since she's been back at school."

"But I'm sure she's already had more than a few experiences. I remember when I turned twelve, it was as if a whole new world had opened up to me. And the number of heads I turned—"

"That's great, Mom," Gemma cut in. "But I want to hear about how Ivy is doing *aside* from her new powers. I haven't seen her since the start of summer."

She sent her cousin a grateful look.

"So, how's school going, Ivy? Did you get the good English teacher, or are you stuck with boring Ms. Powell?" Gemma had also gone to the same school, just six years ahead of her. She was currently in her senior year at the high school and was thankfully giving Ivy pieces of advice along the way.

Ivy smiled. "Fawn and I got Mr. Ashwell, but Alec got stuck with Ms. Powell."

"How is that possible? Aren't they twins?"

"Yep. But I think they were doing every other name? I'm not totally sure, though." It wasn't as if she knew how a middle school teacher's mind worked. Much less some of the crazy ones at *her* middle school.

Grace nodded impatiently. "I'm sure Ivy is doing fine in school academically. She always has. That's not news anymore. Have you been on any dates recently?"

Could she lie to a relative? Her hesitation must have been answer enough because Grace smiled a combination of smugness and pride, as if Ivy's dating life were somehow a reflection on her.

"Just two dates."

"With different boys?"

"The same one."

This caught Gemma's attention. "Is it Alec?"

"What? No! Of course not. Alec has been a pain in the ass recently, actually. I thought we used to bicker before, but now it's like we can't even have a conversation without pissing one another off. And I *try* not to since I know it puts Fawn in a bad position, but I've been so tempted to smack him a few times that it's a wonder I haven't yet."

Gemma and Grace shared a smile. They rarely agreed on things, and when they did, God help whoever opposed them.

"What?" Ivy demanded.

Grace leaned forward. "You've known him for almost four years now, right?"

"Yes." Why were they asking this? They knew that Leila had taken them right to the Belgraves after they left Greece.

"And you've never felt this intense urge to... *argue* with him?"

Ivy didn't like where this was headed. "Not like this."

Gemma seemed to sense her discomfort and despite seeming as excited as her mom, piped up, "Mom, maybe we shouldn't—"

"Have you stopped to consider that maybe Alec is your soulmate?"

If Ivy had been drinking water, she would have spit it out in her cousin's face, and maybe dropped an expensive crystal cup. "Are you kidding me? Of course not. Wouldn't I know by now?"

Grace now had a gleam in her eye. "Not necessarily."

"Leila, we were just talking to Ivy. Tell us more about that Alec Belgrave, would you?"

"Another time, Grace," Leila answered, poking her head out of the kitchen. "Ivy, I need you to help me with more hors d'oeuvres."

Ivy knew it was a lie, but she wasn't about to throw back the life-saver her mom had given her. "Be right there."

Inside the kitchen, Leila said, "Grace giving you a hard time?"

"Gemma tried to help."

"That's nice, but it doesn't change how trying my dear cousin can be. She's just excited for you."

Ivy sighed. "I know. But she also has *no* concept of personal boundaries. I doubt even a t-shirt that said, 'No questions at this time,' would hold her off. And she kept fixating on my saying that Alec and I have been arguing more. And *then* she said he was probably my soulmate. What is that all about?"

Leila didn't say anything for a moment. "She's not wrong." She pointed to the oven. "When that dings, please take it out and bring some over to Brendan. He's been asking about them constantly ever since he walked in." Her mother left leaving her to stew alone.

"Sure," Ivy said automatically, still trying to digest what her mom had just said. *Alec* was her soulmate. Holy shit.

This was why she and Fawn disagreed about family gatherings. There was always someone bound to say something that should have stayed unsaid and left a mess behind.

TWO WEEKS LATER, ALEC TURNED THE PAGE IN his copy of *The Amber Spyglass* and fought back a yawn. He'd loved *The Golden Compass*, but the third book was driving him to nap rather than read. But that was still better than sitting and doing nothing but wait for Fawn and Ivy to be ready. *And* it was nice to break his reading slump since he'd barely touched his bookshelf over the summer.

Why did girls take so long to get ready? Make up, a dress, and shoes? How much did all of that *really* take? He stood up and walked around. He bet most of it was actually them just talking and losing track of time. That had to be the only explanation.

"Are you almost done in there?" he called through the door.

"Calm down!" Fawn replied. "You've only been waiting for twenty minutes. Don't be so melodramatic."

He heard them continue a conversation and heard Ivy say, "because he asked me when no one else did."

Wait. Were they talking about her date? And why hadn't he asked her to go with him? As a friend, obviously. But still, it would have been easier for everyone since they were already going as a group and meeting their dates there. He shook his head. It didn't matter now.

The door opened and there stood Fawn and Ivy. Ivy wore a green dress that made him wonder if she'd ever looked that good before, but he honestly couldn't recall another time that she wore such a pretty color.

"Are you going to move so we can leave?"

He quickly moved out of their way, wishing he had returned to the couch and his boring book when he'd had the chance.

TWO HOURS INTO THE PARTY, IVY'S FEET WERE killing her. She should have listened to Fawn when they were getting ready. She clearly wasn't at the same stage as the rest of her female relatives, who practically lived in heels. Although it wasn't her fault she didn't want to be click-clacking all over the place in her middle school's hallways. The teachers were grumpy enough about students being loud during the measly five minutes they had between class. She had no doubt they'd be eager to complain about someone wearing heels, too.

Everyone's eyes had been on her since she entered with Alec and Fawn. When she was younger and wanted to be the center of attention, she had thought it was the best place to be. Now she knew how wrong she was. Being under the constant gaze of the guys who looked at her like she was their next meal, and their dates who looked like they wouldn't mind knocking her out, made her ready to jump out of her skin. Which was impossible in these shoes that made it hard to walk and sway.

She tried to focus on Beck, her date for the night who had been nothing but a gentleman, but also shared zero chemistry with her. It wasn't his fault that she wasn't as interested in him as he clearly was in her. Over his shoulder, she saw Fawn dancing and laughing with Dylan. She was really happy for her friend, but was it wrong to be a little bit jealous of her, too?

"I'll be right back, okay?" she told him.

The moment he let his hands fall from her waist, she made a bee-line for Fawn. "Hey, Dylan. Mind if I steal her for a second? Thanks."

"She's all yours. I'll get some punch."

"Ivy, what's up?" Fawn asked.

"I need to get out of here. Are you ready to go?"

"Um..." her friend thought out loud, making Ivy feel like a jerk for cutting Fawn's date short. "Let me just go and say goodbye to Dylan. I'll meet you and Alec at the exit. And if you could distract him that would be amazing. I think Dylan might kiss me."

"You haven't kissed yet?"

Fawn shook her head. "Okay, see you in a bit."

Ivy watched her reunite with Dylan and take the plastic cup from him. She didn't miss how disappointed he looked. Fawn was definitely a better friend than her right now. She looked away to give them privacy and searched for Alec. He stood alone by the wall on the other side of the gymnasium. His date was nowhere to be seen. "Fawn and I were going to head back soon."

"Okay," he said, staring at the crowded dance floor.

"Do you want to say goodbye to your date?"

He shook his head. "She only came here with me to make Scott jealous. Don't know why that worked, but it did."

Ivy felt her stomach tighten at his name but didn't say anything.

"Where's Fawn?"

"Saying goodbye to Dylan. She said to meet her by the exit."

He pushed off the wall and put on his jacket. "Let's go."

Clearly, she wasn't the only one over the dance.

A few moments later, Fawn ran over to them with a slight smile and less-subtle glow. She seemed to be the only one who enjoyed the dance. Thankfully, Alec seemed oblivious and walked in front of them.

Fawn whispered, "Did he see?"

"No. I didn't even see."

"WHAT MOVIE? PLEASE DON'T MAKE IT *THE NOTEBOOK*, I beg you." Alec pointed to the screen. "What'll it be?"

"Anything but a rom-com," Ivy said.

"The newest superhero one?" Fawn suggested.

"I'm cool with that. Ivy?"

"Fine with me. I'm going to change." She went into Fawn's room.

"Me, too," his sister said.

He watched them go and wondered why they hadn't changed when he had. Their dresses couldn't be more comfortable than his suit, and yet they had stayed in theirs until *after* they ordered in dinner and picked their movie for the night. He shook his head. *Girls.* He'd never understand them.

He got up and made three plates for them, equal parts of chicken marsala, eggplant parmigiana, and spaghetti marinara, and brought them to the coffee table before individually bringing over the side tables so they could each eat during the movie. Then he waited for them to come back out.

Fawn sat in her normal spot on the opposite side of the couch from him, leaving Ivy to take the seat between them. For some reason, Alec was much more aware of how close Ivy was going to be than he ever had been before. *Who cares? It's not like she hasn't sat next to you before.* And while that was true, Alec still couldn't shake his fixation on that small detail.

"Took you long enough," he said, hitting play on the remote.

They ate and watched in silence. Once they were done with their food, they paused the movie and demolished a tub of caramel ice cream. When the movie was over, Fawn put their bowls into the sink. "I'm exhausted. Ivy, come in whenever you want. I'll leave the light on for you."

Alec glanced at Ivy when she didn't immediately scoot away. In fact, she was practically leaning into him. "Ivy?" he asked, unsure of what she wanted. He knew what *he* wanted.

She didn't answer. At least, not out loud. Her steady focus on his lips gave him all the hint he needed before he closed the distance and pressed his lips to hers. Her hands came up to hold his face and he cupped the back of her neck before he felt the sudden urge to kiss more than her mouth.

Unnerved by the intensity of his emotions, he said, "Goodnight, Ivy." Then, like a coward, he retreated into his bedroom.

The next morning, Ivy sat at the kitchen table with Fawn. Stella stood at the counter looking through her planner when Alec finally emerged from his room.

"Hey, sleepyhead," Stella said. "What do you want for breakfast?"

He plopped himself into the seat next to Fawn and across from Ivy. "Whatever they're having, please." It was probably covered in sugar and this morning he found himself needing the extra kick. His dreams last night kept replaying the kiss and he had woken up exhausted.

Stella proved him right by placing a bowl of oatmeal—if it could even still be considered that—covered in sugar. It was topped with fruit, and there was a smoothie to accompany it, but he could almost feel himself getting a cavity just from staring at it. He closed his eyes and dug in.

When he opened his eyes, he saw Ivy watching him and tried to decipher her expression. Would she say anything about the kiss? Did she want *him* to? He wasn't sure he wanted to advertise it in front of his mom and sister. Not when he still wasn't sure what it meant. And what it meant for him and Ivy. And besides, if Ivy really wanted Fawn to know, he'd hear about it from his sister soon after.

It was settled. He wouldn't say anything now and let Ivy talk about it when she was ready. He congratulated himself on coming to the well-thought-out conclusion, but when Ivy left soon after the meal without saying so much as a word to him or sparing him another glance, he wondered if he'd made an irreparable mistake instead.

CHAPTER 6

9 YEARS LATER

Ivy watched her mom, a few of their cousins who were visiting from Greece, Alec, Fawn, and Stella raise their glasses to her. "Happy birthday, Ivy!"

They each took a sip of the champagne. Ivy saw Fawn make a face, but quickly recover.

"Thank you so much!"

"It's not every day you turn twenty-one, is it?" her mother asked. She addressed Alec and Fawn. "Don't worry, your birthday is coming soon. Luckily, I was able to convince the restaurant's owners to allow everyone to drink."

Her female cousins and Stella chuckled at that while the men shook their heads, amused smiles curving their mouths. Her friends smiled, but she knew by their vacant expressions that they had no idea what was so funny.

"Is it a family joke?" Fawn asked.

Ivy nodded and smiled at her family. She just hoped none of them would be too obvious in their curiosity about Alec.

He made a *hmph* sound and took another sip of his champagne while staring at the white table cloth in front of him.

Ivy narrowed her eyes at him. "Oh, like I didn't have to sit through your family's inside jokes when we first met?"

He opened his mouth, closed it, then replied, "Oh, give me a break. We were only eight years-old!"

Fawn met her gaze and they rolled their eyes at him.

"Hey..." He pointed between them. "That's not fair. You're always teaming up against me."

"Well, duh," Fawn said, elbowing him in the side. "It's the only way we can stay sane around you."

Ivy saw he was about to retort when her cousin Brendan said, "Hey, Alec. They giving you trouble over there?"

Alec shook his head. "This is barely anything compared to what they normally do."

"Us guys have to stick together against all the estrogen in the room."

Ivy stared at Alec, daring him to agree.

He met her gaze and cleared his throat. "I'm good. They may be a pain in my ass, but I love them anyway."

"*Sure* you do. You love Ivy just like family, right?"

Oh, he was *not* going to drop that bombshell on Alec tonight on her birthday—or ever. Just because he was older than her didn't mean he got a free pass to do whatever he wanted. "Give it a rest, Brendan," Ivy called down the table.

He lifted his glass to her in a mock-salute. "Whatever you say, little cousin." He winked at her and turned back to his conversation with their other cousin who had just started law school.

She turned to see Alec and Fawn staring at her, the same silent question in their twin eyes. She rolled her eyes, hoping they'd realize Brendan was just joking and drop the topic. Alec dropped his gaze, but Fawn didn't.

Ivy gestured to the bathroom and her best friend nodded. When they stood up together, Stella met her gaze and smiled. She smiled back. She wasn't sure if Stella knew, but she had a feeling she approved.

The moment Fawn closed the bathroom door, she turned and said, "Okay, spill. What was Brendan going on about?"

"I... may have a small crush on your brother—but *don't* tell him," Ivy added the last part when she saw her friend break out into an excited smile.

"I won't, but why won't you tell him?"

"He sees me just as your best friend. I'm sure I'm just another sister in his eyes."

Fawn looked away.

"What?"

"Well, I'm sure that's mostly true. But there are times when I see him looking at you when you're not looking."

Ivy felt hope bloom in her chest but tamped down the emotion. "I'm not ready."

Fawn pulled her into a hug. "It's up to you."

"Thank you."

A LEC SAT UP WHEN HIS SISTER AND IVY returned. He knew they had been talking about something personal, or they wouldn't have minded saying it in front of him.

Fawn looked happy and it looked like Ivy was blushing. He looked to his sister, but she shook her head. *Dammit.* He wanted to know why.

"Breathe, Alec," his sister whispered, "or you'll break your glass."

He loosened his grip on the thin stem and leaned back in his seat.

Ivy gave him a small smile before she was pulled into a conversation by a female cousin sitting near her. He couldn't hear their conversation, but he saw the cousin briefly look at him while they talked. It made the hair on the back of his neck stand up. Why was almost everyone in Ivy's family giving him looks like that today?

Leila spoke up. "Alec, I was wondering what your plans were for the rest of summer before you start Junior year."

"Oh, well, I'm working part time at a coffee shop. Just making some money before homework and classes eat up most of my time."

She nodded. "And do you meet interesting people there?"

"Not really. But there are some regulars who I've gotten to know."

She leaned forward and rested her elbows on the table. "Any cute girls you've slipped your number to with their order?"

He suddenly felt like his shirt's collar was too tight. Why did this feel different when she'd asked about his dating life when they were younger? He didn't have time to think about it more before *someone* kicked his shin. "No, no one that I can think of off the top of my head."

The waiter came by to talk to Leila and Alec took the opportunity to kick his sister back and growl, "What the hell was that for?"

"Didn't want to you to ruin Ivy's birthday celebration."

"Give me some credit."

He sensed Ivy watching him and turned just in time to see her paste on a fake smile. He still didn't know why she had that reaction, but it made him feel like a jerk.

He opened his mouth to apologize when the lights went out and everyone started singing Happy Birthday. A vanilla cake with sea foam green frosting appeared. He joined in.

Later, when people were getting ready to leave, he walked over to Ivy. She smiled, but he could tell it wasn't her usual, genuine one. "Look, I'm sorry about earlier—"

"It's okay. I know my mom put you in an awkward position."

"So, are we good? I can't leave knowing I upset the birthday girl."

She pulled him in for a hug and he quickly wrapped his arms around her. "I could never stay mad at you," she said quietly.

He didn't respond at first, just enjoyed holding her. Then he stepped back and gave her a mischievous grin. "I'll remember you said that the next time I piss you off."

She pushed him off and glared, but he could tell she wasn't angry or upset anymore.

"Happy birthday, Ivy. I hope it's a great year for you."

"Thank you. I do, too."

Her somewhat strange response stuck with him even as he fell asleep that night.

I VY SMILED AT RÁMON'S WILDLY INAPPROPRIATE AND SOMEWHAT sexist joke. But leave it to his charming Paraguayan accent to make it something to laugh at. His humor was probably the thing she liked best about him. Although his good looks weren't bad either.

Her other female friends seemed to agree. Since the party had started, they had ogled him, along with most of her other male friends that she'd invited. She had to admit, they were a group of fine-looking men. The roof looked more like a frat party than a birthday, but she didn't mind.

"Let's hear it for the birthday girl, Ivy Moore!" Jackson shouted from the other side of the roof pool. He stood on one of the pool chairs and shot a fist pump into the air, making her smile. He always was a loud one, but she loved that about him.

She lifted her piña colada in a mock-salute, took a sip, then handed it to Fawn before she dove into the cool water. Despite being a fire sign, she *did* love water. Whether it be a beach near an ocean, a lake, or even a man-made pool, she felt unbelievably happy. The heat was killer today, which made swimming feel that much better. She did four laps and pulled herself out of the water. Railings and stairs were for wusses.

Fawn smiled at her. "I think every guy here just lost their minds watching you."

Ivy shrugged. That wasn't news. "If they want to look, I won't complain. But that was completely for *my* entertainment, not theirs."

"I wish I was more like you. I don't get how you're so confident around guys."

If only her best friend knew what she was really saying. "You just have to remember they're probably as nervous as you."

"You make it sound so easy."

Ivy held Fawn's shoulders. "Just because you haven't had a boyfriend since Dylan moved after high school doesn't mean you'll never have another."

"I know that. It just sucks in the meantime."

She surveyed the guys crowding the roof. *Believe me, I know.*

A LEC WATCHED IVY AND FAWN ON THE OTHER side of the pool and desperately wished he knew how to magically amplify his hearing. But since Fawn was given the family Grimoire, he had no idea where to start. *What were they talking about?* It must have been funny because his sister threw her head back. Even if he couldn't hear her laughing, he knew that she was.

A guy stood next to him and also watched them. If he was looking at his sister... Alec held out his hand. "Hi, I'm Alec. And you are?"

"Jackson." The guy had a firm handshake.

"How do you know the birthday girl?"

"We dated a few months ago."

Whoever said surprises were a thing of joy was an idiot. Alec swallowed the lump in his throat. "And you're still friends, I take it."

"Yeah. I'm really glad, too. She's just so great, you know? I'd hate to give up being around her just because we broke up."

Was this guy still in love with her? "So, it was a mutual decision?"

Jackson hesitated, and Alec had his answer. "No, but I can see now that she was right. She's a lot more social than I am. I mean, I go to some parties and events with the team, but she lives for going out. Not that I'm saying that's a bad thing," he quickly added as if criticizing Ivy was wrong.

"Of course not. Excuse me."

Now that Ivy was off talking to other guests, Alec made a beeline for his sister who was now sipping her own piña colada.

"Does that have alcohol in it?"

Fawn pointed at him. "Before you give me a lecture about it, big brother, it's Ivy's party and her mom got the hotel staff to let all attendees enjoy a wet bar."

"So, the answer is yes?"

She nodded. He grabbed the drink from her hand and downed it in three large gulps, ignoring the brain freeze that immediately attacked him. He put the empty glass on a table and said, "I'll get you a new one." Then he pushed his way to the bar, ordered her another and himself a glass of water. Five minutes later, he sat down next to her again.

Fawn raised her eyebrows at him. "What was *that* about?"

He ignored her question and sat next to her. "I just met Jackson."

His sister's face turned into one of understanding and then pity.

That wasn't encouraging. "How many of Ivy's exes are here?"

Fawn surveyed the other guests for a few moments. "About thirty."

There were only one-hundred guests. He scanned the crowd, mentally counting. "That's all the guys here." *Holy shit.* "I think I'm going to go."

"Come on, Alec, don't go. She's friends with her exes, so what?"

Although the news made him feel slightly better, it wasn't enough. "Would you tell Ivy I left?"

Ivy seemed to have heard them because she came toward them. "Wait, you're leaving already?"

"Yeah, I'm sorry I have to duck out early. But it's a great party." He kissed her cheek. "Happy birthday again, Ivy."

"Are you leaving, too?" she asked Fawn.

"No, she's staying," he answered for his sister. "Please make sure she doesn't get into too much trouble."

"As if *I'd* be the one out of the two of us to get into trouble," Fawn retorted. "I'll see you later," she added more gently, clearly still feeling sorry for him.

He waved goodbye to them and left the roof pool. Once inside the hotel's stainless-steel elevator, he closed his eyes and prayed that chugging his sister's drink wouldn't come back to bite him in the ass with a hangover later. He seemed to share his sister's lightweight nature—something he definitely could have done without. In the lobby, he called a ride, wanting nothing more than to close his eyes and sleep.

Maybe that would make today better. Or maybe not. But it couldn't make things worse.

CHAPTER 7

1 MONTH LATER

FAWN FIXED HER WITH A SKEPTICAL LOOK. "YOU say it's going to be fun every time. And it *never* is for me."

"I promise this time will be different."

Her best friend rolled her eyes. "I'm not going tonight. I have to work on a group project, three papers, and two presentations."

"And *that* is why I'm glad I'm not an English major like you."

"Women's Studies also gives you lots of papers."

Ivy waved her objection off. "I could write those in my sleep."

"Wouldn't that be a nice power to have," she heard Fawn mumble.

"So, you're really not going with me tonight?"

Her roommate shook her head. "But go anyway. I know you'll have a good time. Maybe even a better one since I won't be the downer you have to watch."

Ivy sat down on her friend's bed. "You know I hate when you talk about yourself like that. Your self-esteem doesn't stand a chance against you. So, cut it out."

"Yes, *Mom*. Now, go already. And don't worry about me."

Although Ivy wasn't an introvert like Fawn, she still needed down time every now and then. Too bad her siren nature didn't seem to care. Tonight, she was so restless and in need of energy, staying in the dorm wasn't an option.

She started the fifteen-minute walk to Greek Row and cursed the school for not allowing Greek Life on campus. Any time someone wanted to party, they had to walk down a road that was so dark it made the Haunted Forest in *The Wizard of Oz* look friendly. She clutched her phone in her pocket with the safety app open, her finger on the screen to alert Fawn automatically if her fingerprint went away.

When she reached the entrance, she pulled out her phone, turned off the app, and hung her coat up in the frat President's bedroom closet, away from the giant pile in the house's living room. She'd be lying if she said she hadn't used some of her Supernatural abilities to get special treatment now and then.

"Ivy!"

She smiled and hugged Patrick. "Hey!" He was one of the few who she hadn't hooked up with. And probably never would since he was interested in the same type of people she was. "How's your boyfriend? Is he here?"

"No. He's visiting family this weekend."

"Aw, and he left you all alone?" She patted his arm.

"It gets worse. I'm the sober ride for these jokers tonight."

Yikes. "Well, at least you'll stay busy."

"And so will you, I bet." He gave an exaggerated wink, making her laugh. "Let me get you a drink."

"I'm good tonight. Thanks, though." She was already feeling a bit lightheaded from all the energy in the building. "I'm just going to go dance for now."

He nodded. "Happy hunting!"

She saluted him and entered the fray of the dance floor in the basement. She greeted some of the other brothers and let the music move through her. It was a throwback themed party which meant there was no music from the current year, or last few years, for that matter. Which was fine with her since she liked almost anything. She'd even grown to enjoy musical theater albums thanks to Fawn.

She felt the sexual energy rising from the crowd of dancing bodies and let it permeate her, both energizing and calming the restlessness that plagued her more often than not. Feeling someone watching her, she turned and saw a guy dancing next to her. "I'm Ivy."

"Landon," he replied. "You're really good at dancing. I can't keep my eyes off you."

She moved closer, facing him so her chest almost brushed his. "You really think so?"

He smiled down at her. "Now you're just fishing for compliments."

She turned her head and flipped her hair over her shoulder. "I would never."

"I don't believe that for a second."

"That hurts my feelings, Landon. You can make it up to me by dancing with me for the next few songs. If you behave, maybe I'll extend that cut-off."

"Isn't that what we're already doing?"

She laughed. "Not even close." She reached down between them and took his hands in hers. She turned her back to him and placed one of his hands on her hip and the other on her stomach before reaching back and cupping his neck, pulling his head down to hers. "*Now* we're dancing," she said, rolling her hips to the new beat.

He groaned, and his hands tightened on her body as he began dancing behind her, following the rhythm she set. They danced like that for the next three songs and Ivy let herself bask in his lustful attention.

Then someone said loudly, "Get away from her!" Before she knew it, she was pulled away from Landon and saw a clearly-drunk Jackson glaring at him.

Her dance partner said, "What's your problem, man?"

Jackson took a menacing step forward, so Ivy quickly freed herself from his grasp and inserted herself between the two. She placed a hand on his chest and felt how fast his heart was beating. Not only that, a thick cloud of red surrounded him. "Jackson? Jackson!" His gaze finally focused on her, clearing the anger from his eyes. "What's going on?"

Now that the anger was gone, he just looked sadder than she'd ever seen him. He went to his knees and wrapped his arms around her waist and said, "Ivy, I'm miserable without you. Please, take me back!"

She gently pried him off. "Jackson, what's gotten into you?"

"I just can't go on without you. I miss you so much."

"Jackson," she whispered, "I don't feel that way about you anymore."

He fell back a step, looking devastated. "Oh, okay. Sorry to bother you, Ivy."

"Jackson..." She took a step forward, but he put his hands up.

"I'm good, Ivy. I hope you have a good night."

She watched him go and wondered if she should follow him. But wouldn't that send a mixed message? *That* didn't seem like a good idea.

She felt someone's hand on her arm and practically jumped out of her skin. The energy was no longer comforting, but suffocating. "Are you okay?"

Ivy turned back to Landon and forced a smile. "No, but I will be. Just a little rattled, is all. I'm sure you can understand why."

He nodded. "I don't think anyone wants to run into their ex. But I have to say, you handled that pretty well. And since I have to give credit where it's due, your ex did too. Well, once he calmed down."

She patted his arm. "Look, I really like you, but I think I'm going to go home tonight. Do you have your phone on you?"

"Yeah." He reached into his pocket and handed it to her.

She put in her number and said, "I'll see you around then."

W*HAT THE HELL?* ALEC SHOT UP IN BED and pulled down his shirt to see his necklace glowing bright, creating a circle of light where it lay against his skin. *What did it mean?* His mom had said that it would amplify his twin connection to Fawn, but he'd never actually had it activate before. Not even when she cried her eyes out when Dylan had broken up with her.

He checked his phone and saw that it was the middle of the night and sighed even as he speed-dialed his sister. "Hey, sis. What's happening over there? My necklace burned me."

He heard crying, then his sister answered, sounding equally tired. "Sorry. We're just having a tough night over here."

"What happened?"

She sighed, and he heard her muffled voice ask Ivy something. "Our university President just emailed everyone to tell us Jackson died tonight. Ivy's really upset. You remember meeting him, right?"

"Yeah." He took a deep breath. "Is she okay?" And did she still have feelings for him? Was that why she was so upset?

As if reading his mind, Fawn said, "I know what you're thinking. The answer is no. She just saw him at a party last night and he died while driving back to his dorm drunk after he begged her to take him back. Ivy feels like it's her fault he left."

"She has to know it's not her fault."

"I've been telling her that since she got back, but she's inconsolable right now. I just bought enough ice cream to fuel three break ups. I don't know when she'll be okay again."

Alec felt his chest clench in sympathy for Ivy. "Well, I'm so sorry to hear that happened, and please keep me updated on how you're doing."

She yawned. "Will do, Alec. I'm going to say goodnight. Sorry again about waking you up."

"Good night, sis." He hung up and stared at his ceiling, trying to force his mind to go blank. A student had died, which was obviously upsetting. He just hoped Ivy and Fawn would feel better soon. He knew how sensitive they were, and this couldn't be easy on them. And Ivy may have dated Jackson, but if Fawn was right, things were over between them. He rubbed his hand down his face and cursed. *Well, great.* Now he'd be up for at least another hour before he fell asleep again. Luckily, he didn't have class until late morning. That still didn't make him feel any better, though.

Ivy stared up at her ceiling. She hadn't been able to fall asleep until three in the morning, leaving her with only five measly hours of sleep.

There was a knock on her bedroom door.

"Come in," she called.

Fawn walked in. "I just wanted to make sure you were awake. I know you have class in an hour."

"I know. But I don't think I have the energy to go."

"Okay. Do you need anything from me?"

"No. But thank you for offering."

Fawn hovered in the doorway, then came over to her bed. "I think you should get dressed. It might make you feel better. I know that helps me when I'm feeling low on energy. Anyway, I have to go to class, but text me if you need me to get you anything while I'm out. Will I see you at lunch later today?"

"Sure." It would give her something to do, otherwise she'd stay inside all day.

Once the door closed behind Fawn, Ivy slowly pushed herself up to a sitting position and tried to convince her body to fully stand. It just felt like the smallest action now took Herculean effort. Part of it, she knew was being physically exhausted, but it was also the emotional impact of Jackson's death.

Ivy couldn't shake the feeling that she did play a pivotal role in how his night played out. She wasn't sure how it was possible, but she was convinced her siren powers motivated his weird behavior.

She took a deep breath, pushed off her bed and got dressed. Moping forever wasn't productive, and she'd feel only worse about herself if her academics took a direct hit because of something she *logically* knew was out of her control.

A LEC HELD HIS PHONE TO HIS EAR, "Is she doing any better?" His sister's hesitation had him wishing he hadn't asked.

She looked down at her hands which was never a good sign. "Yes."

"But?" There had to be more.

"Well," his sister started, looking back up at the screen. "She definitely seems to be doing better."

He wanted to reach through the phone and shake his sister. He knew when she was stalling, and this was one of those times. "Just tell me how she's doing, Fawn."

"She's going out again."

"Okay. That's good, right?"

"I guess. It's what she normally does, so I'd normally say yes..." Her voice lifted at the end, indicating she really didn't want to say whatever came next.

"But?" he prompted.

Her next words came out in a rush. "But she's going through guys so fast here, it's like nothing I've ever seen before. It's like some intimacy switch went off in her mind after Jackson died."

His stomach tightened at the idea of Ivy having so many flings. College guys weren't exactly known for being upstanding guys. "Is she being safe?"

"Of course, she is. She always texts me when she gets to a guy's place, tells me who he is and his phone number, and also calls when she's on her way back."

"Even in the middle of the night?"

"Well, no. She texts if it's really late."

"But what if she got into trouble and you were sleeping?"

"Alec, we have it under control. We have a whole system and have had it since freshman year. We're good."

"You can't blame me for worrying about both of you."

She leaned forward. "No, I can't. But I promise we're fine. I have to go."

The call shut off and he stared at his blank screen for a moment, still absorbing what Fawn had said about Ivy. He was glad she was getting back to normal, but he'd be lying if he pretended to be happy about her uptick in number of exes. It always made him feel a little jealous when he heard about her relationships, but he mostly ignored it. She was her own person who could do what she wanted. And as his sister pointed out, neither of them needed saving either. And if they did, they had each other.

But even with all that being true, he still needed to blow off some energy or he'd end up snapping at Fawn or Ivy the next time he talked to one of them. He may be a little hotheaded at times, but he was smart enough to now know how to avoid explosive conversations. For the most part, that is.

Pulling out his phone, he opened the contacts app and his thumb hovered over the name of the girl who'd slipped him enough hints during their last study group that he knew he'd be able to stop thinking for the afternoon. He clicked her name and texted her: *Is your offer still on the table?*

She immediately sent back: *When should I come over?*

CHAPTER 8

Ivy checked her watch and blew out an impatient breath. Why was the train *always* late? If Fawn had been with her, they would be joking about it. But her best friend was busy binge-watching the latest season of her favorite TV show on her laptop.

She felt someone watching her and turned to see a college-aged guy standing a little down the platform from her. She gave him a small smile, but didn't maintain eye-contact for long. She wasn't going to encourage that type of attention. Not until she got to spend time with her family and got more answers.

Ivy felt the vibrations before she saw the train's lights. She picked up her bag and tapped her foot as the passengers departed. When the entrance closest to her cleared, she grabbed a seat and plugged in her laptop.

The conductor came. He held a scanner in one hand and held the other out. "Ticket, please."

Ivy turned the brightness up on her phone and held it up to him. "Thank you."

She was just turning on her wireless headphones when she noticed the guy from the platform had grabbed a seat across the aisle from her. This time, she didn't look his way. Instead, she hooked into the train's WiFi and messaged her mom that she was waiting to depart. She put on her favorite artist's new album.

Three hours, one nap, and five pages later, her train pulled into Grand Central Station. Ivy packed up her things and walked with the throng of commuters through the underground tunnels to the subway. She sat down in between two women. She noticed that one was reading a popular romance novel. Ivy made a mental note to buy a copy once she got home.

By the time Ivy was turning her key in the lock, all she wanted to do was nap. She would talk to her mom later. But when she opened the door, she was surprised to see her aunt and cousins filling their living room's furniture.

"Ivy, you're here. Say hello."

"Hi, everyone. I'll be right back." She walked into her bedroom and dropped her bag on her bed. She changed into a pair of sweatpants and sweater. When she came back out, she sat next to her mom. "I didn't know you were coming over."

Gemma spoke up. "We knew you were only going to be here for a few days."

"And we couldn't pass up the opportunity to hear about how school is going," Brendan added.

Ivy looked over at her mom, who shook her head. "Well, one of my friends died a few weeks ago. I'm pretty sure I was partly responsible."

His friendly expression dropped. "Oh my God. I'm so sorry, Ivy."

She just nodded. What else could she do? She still didn't have the answers she needed to do anything else. "I saw him the night he died." She hadn't been able to tell her mom over the phone. Maybe it was a form of denial, but telling her mom brought her fears that she *was* somehow responsible crashing down on her.

"I thought you had moved on from him."

"I had. I ran into him at a party and he was acting really strange. He begged me to take him back. He was practically desperate. I'd never seen him act like that before."

"And you think you caused it."

Even though her mom hadn't phrased it as a question, Ivy confirmed it, "Yes."

Gemma caught her gaze. "There's something else, isn't there?"

That got her mother's attention. "Is she right, Ivy?" No one said anything, waiting for her to answer.

When she didn't speak up, her mom repeated herself more firmly. "Have you been feeding regularly?"

Ivy didn't answer immediately. "Yes."

"Ivy." She couldn't miss the reprimand in her mom's tone.

"I don't do it every day if that's what you're asking. I haven't been since he died. I go out about three times a week. Or I just go when I start feeling restless. I guess I've been intermittently fasting?"

No one smiled at her joke. Not that she expected them to. She knew it wasn't funny. Her feeling sick all the time certainly wasn't something she found amusing. But what else could she say? What defined a "regular diet"? It wasn't like there was a siren's eating plan she could follow. She couldn't help but laugh inwardly at that. She tried imagining a cheesy book cover with the title, *The Everyday Siren's Balanced Diet: How to Thrive On Land, In Sea, and Everything In Between.*

"And then I've been going to the other extreme and going through multiple guys a night," she continued. She may have been more sexual than Fawn and most of her other classmates since puberty, but she had never gone *this* far before.

Her mom made a *tsk*-ing sound. "That explains it. You need to feed more regularly, daily, if possible. If you're feeling on edge, you're already starved for more energy and your powers kick into overdrive and pump the people around you for more, so you can satisfy your appetite faster. The only thing that helps is one's soulmate."

It was the confirmation she needed, but it only made her feel worse. "So, it is my fault Jackson wasn't in his right mind. He never would have drunk so much or driven home while intoxicated if my powers weren't making him crazy."

"You didn't know, Ivy. Prolonged exposure to us can sometimes have adverse side effects like aggression, but normally nothing bad happens. You're *not* responsible for his death."

"How can you know for sure?"

Her mother sighed. "You didn't kill him, Ivy. It was a terrible accident, but that's all it was."

"Okay." What else could she say to that?

A
LEC OPENED HIS DOOR AND PULLED HIS VISITOR into a hug before he could say a word. "It's so great to see you! I feel like it's been forever. How have you been?"

Dylan chuckled. "It's good to see you, too." He patted his back. "Are you going to let me in now?"

Alec let him go, then punched him in the arm. "Jerk."

"Missed you, too, bro. So... no roommate?"

He shook his head. "Too used to having my own room." Luckily, his mom had never made him and Fawn share one.

"I'm sure it's nice not having to lock anyone out when you have a date."

Alec nodded. "Well, I'm sure you know that, too, right?"

His friend shook his head. "Technically, I do, but my dad and I are housing a bunch of family friends for the foreseeable future and they're a little nosy. Hard as hell to be with a girl without one of them knowing and then giving me a hard time afterward."

"And you can't just tell them to mind their own business?"

Dylan shook his head. "Wish it was that simple. Anyway, how's your dining hall's food here? I'm starving."

"Yeah, let's go."

Once they were sitting down, Dylan leaned forward. "What about you? Have a girlfriend yet?"

Alec quickly swallowed his sip of soda and shot his best friend what he hoped was a scathing look. "No."

Dylan shrugged. "You can't blame me for asking. I didn't know if you had gotten together with Ivy since I last saw you."

"We haven't. I don't know why you thought we would. And the only reason we haven't caught up in so long is you kept dropping off the face of the Earth. I wouldn't hear from you for months. What was that about anyway?"

"Got a really bad case of mono."

"Multiple times? Isn't that supposed to not happen?"

His friend shrugged. "Probably just got unlucky. Anyway, what are you doing hanging out with me instead of being at a party?"

Because it was getting boring as hell. All the girls were starting to blend together. Something he would never admit aloud to his sister or Ivy. They'd knock him out before he even finished speaking. And he would deserve it. "We can do that if you want."

Dylan shook his head. "I don't think so. You look like the very idea wants to make you hurl. Speaking of, have you done any boxing lately? We could go for a round or two."

"Ha. That was only the first time. And, no, I haven't." Alec couldn't actually remember the last time he'd gone to the gym. "But I'm happy to prove I can still kick your ass."

Dylan laughed. The bastard. "Maybe you could back in high school, but I've gotten a lot better."

He'd certainly gotten a lot *bigger*. Alec wasn't going to guess how much muscle his friend had put on, but it was nothing to sneeze at. "I don't doubt it. Do you live at the gym now?"

"Nope. But the guys living with us are a bunch of gym rats and I join them whenever I have time."

Alec grabbed his bag, dumped his food, and pointed to Dylan. "Okay, time to show me some new moves."

"Just don't forget to duck."

IVY DROPPED HER BAG ONTO THE FLOOR OF her bedroom then flopped down on the bed. Even though she had just been at home for three days for a long weekend, it felt as though she had *less* energy than when she left on Friday afternoon.

There was a knock on her door.

"Come in," she called out.

Fawn poked her head in. "Hey, how was your mini-vacation?"

"Exhausting." But worth it. She had picked all her family's brains on how to be a siren without any nasty side effects. "What did you do when I was away?"

"Finished one paper, revised another, got halfway through the latest season on Netflix."

"Did you go outside *at all?*"

Her friend rolled her eyes. "More than half of that work was done at the coffee shop or the library, so yes, *Mom*, I did venture beyond our dorm room." She sat in Ivy's desk chair. "Did you tell your mom I said hi?"

Ivy nodded. "I also passed the message along to Gemma, since I saw her."

"Next break, I want to see your family again. I don't think I've seen any of them since your birthday dinner."

"I'll be sure to tell my cousins." Knowing them, they'd be just as excited as Fawn. Mostly because they would make barely-veiled references to their shared Supernatural backgrounds and then later laugh at her best friend's naïveté. To be honest, they were jerks about it, but she understood why they did it. Because as much as her mom told her to respect Stella's decision to not tell Fawn and Alec about their magic until the night they received their powers, she didn't get why Stella ever thought that was a good idea.

Fawn nodded. A beat of silence passed, and Ivy knew what was coming next.

"How are you doing?"

There it was.

"I'm okay. No, really, I am," she insisted when Fawn was about to argue. "I'm finally at the point where I not only *know* that it wasn't my fault, but I also feel it."

Her friend gave a tentative smile. "Well, I'm glad to hear you're doing better. But if you still need someone to talk to, I'm always here."

"Thank you. That means a lot."

She is a mermaid,
But approach her with caution.
Her mind swims at a depth
Most would drown in.

J IRON WORD

CHAPTER 9

"FAWN?" HE DIDN'T HEAR AN ECHO LIKE HE had half-expected. He still didn't know where they were, but he knew it wasn't any place he'd ever been to before. There was a sort of fuzzy quality about the space he couldn't get away from. That, and the fact that his sister was with him despite him knowing she was at school, made him realize he was in a dream.

His sister stood no more than ten feet from him, but he couldn't seem to move toward her to comfort her and wipe the tears streaming from her eyes.

She was crying so much that his feet started to feel wet. He looked down and saw that even in the dark dreamscape that connected them, Fawn had started to fill the floor with her sorrow.

She didn't seem to hear him and when he opened his mouth to ask her what was wrong, the scene disappeared, and he woke up in bed with his body covered in sweat. He threw off the covers, grabbed a towel, and went to shower.

Thinking back on the dream, he tried to figure out what had been wrong with his sister. All he could think was that the last time she'd been that upset, she and Dylan had just broken up because he was moving to New Orleans. Did that mean someone had broken her heart?

He shook his head. That didn't make any sense. How would that even be possible? He knew full well she hadn't dated anyone since

Dylan. The only other time she was that upset was when their grandma died. That made him pause. If he was finally getting a psychic vision like his sister sometimes did, did that mean she was going to lose someone close to her again? Be it through death or break up? And why didn't he know who the dream was about?

It reminded him of their sixteenth birthday when he'd seen some of Fawn's dream before being pushed out. Five years later, on their twenty-first birthday, he, yet again, found himself privy to her dreams where he knew he was seeing something important but didn't fully understand what it was or why. He hated being left in the dark, unable to protect his sister from whatever threat faced her.

W*HO WAS THAT?* IVY WATCHED A GUY SHE'D never seen before walk in front of her into the auditorium. She couldn't quite say what captivated her about him, but she knew that he was somehow different from the other guys in the class. In the school, for that matter. Something told her he might even be Supernatural, but she had no idea *what* he was.

He must have sensed her watching him because he turned around. She saw that he was as beautiful as he was mysterious. And purple eyes? Now *those* were the things dreams were made of. "I'm Caleb," he held out his hand.

She took it. "Ivy."

"Nice to meet you." He held the door open for her, then continued walking up the stairs to where there were still empty seats. As they approached Fawn's seat, she noticed a faint and blurred red line, as it got brighter and sharper, she realized it was connecting her best friend and this mystery guy.

Huh. That was new. When she was younger, her mom had told her about a lot of different cultures' beliefs about soulmates, but one that she'd always liked was the Red Thread of Marriage in Chinese legend. And while she couldn't be a hundred percent certain this was it, she'd be willing to bet it was. Her pace had slowed, and he passed her.

He sat in the only empty seat next to Fawn, which drew her up short for a split second before she decided she'd rather sit and watch them anyway.

"Oh, I'm sorry." He gestured between them. "Did you want to sit together?" He started to rise, but she put a hand on his shoulder, stopping him.

"No, it's fine." As she passed them and sat in the row behind them, she saw Fawn send her a confused look before focusing back on the stranger when he turned to her.

Class passed, and while she did keep her ears open and typed notes absentmindedly on her laptop, her focus was really on the interaction happening in front of her between her best friend and Caleb.

Despite the line pulsing between them, neither of them showed any of the signs she had grown used to seeing between people who were interested in one other. There was no fuzzy pink or deep red surrounding them. They were whispering at the start of class, but they had very quickly lapsed into silence, even as they kept sneaking glances at each other. The only hints of anything between them Ivy saw were ones anyone could see. Her friend was averting her gaze and blushing, and him watching Fawn with intense fascination as if he were trying to mentally catalogue her features.

There were still tell-tale signs that Fawn and Caleb had an electric connection. One of them would move and the other would adjust as if they shared an unspoken dance.

At the end of class, Fawn seemed to be so lost in her thoughts that she left the hall immediately without a glance back. Ivy sat down with her food and texted her: *Are we having lunch?*

Yes, I'm sorry. I'm on my way.

A few minutes later, Fawn sat down across from her.

Ivy examined her and crossed her arms. "In all the years I've known you, I never took you for a rabbit."

"What is that supposed to mean?"

"What else would you call that back there? Because I call that running scared."

"He's—" Fawn cleared her throat. "He's intense."

"And incredibly hot."

Her friend blushed. "I'm going to go get something to eat."

Ivy waved her off. "You might want to put some ice in your drink. Maybe it'll help cool you down. You look a little flushed there."

Fawn turned around and flipped her off, making her laugh. Hanging out with her and college had definitely made her best friend more assertive than before.

That night, Ivy was sitting at the most popular student bar in the city. The line was out the door when she had arrived but being a regular had it's perks. As did being a siren.

She swirled the remains of her cocktail in front of her.

"Would you like another?"

Ivy turned and saw a guy sit down next to her. He was familiar, but she couldn't remember from which class she had seen him. She almost rejected the offer. If she was going to be spending a lot of time around him, he was officially in her newly-established no-fly zone. She didn't need to repeat any of her old mistakes. *But* the annoyingly persistent, and increasing, incompleteness she felt around Fawn and Caleb made her say the exact opposite. "Yes, I would. Thank you."

He got the bartender's attention. "Another drink for the lady and a beer for me. Whatever's on tap." He turned back to her. "My name is Erik. And you're Ivy, right?"

She smiled. "Yep. I'm sorry, but I know you're in one of my classes, I just can't remember which one."

"No worries. We're in Sexism in the 21st Century together."

Ivy took a drink from her empty glass, only tasting melted ice. "Of course! How could I have forgotten?"

"It's okay, I don't exactly make a huge impression."

She shook her head. "Don't say that."

He tilted his head to the side, eyeing her. "What would you have me say instead?"

"Whatever you want."

"Alright. In that case, I'll ask if after this drink, would you like to get out of here?"

She lifted her drink in silent salute and tipped it back, swallowing half the contents in one go. If she was going to have any fun tonight, she needed some liquid courage.

One drink turned into another, and the more each of them drank, the stronger the cloud of red surrounding him became. If it had been a physical entity, she had no doubt they'd both have trouble breathing. She wasn't sure when it first appeared, but it was definitely there now. Ivy had stopped tracking the minute details of effect her magic had on guys a few years back. She knew the gist of it enough to survive, and that was what mattered. No sooner had she finished her drink did he speak up.

"Let's go."

She touched his arm. "I'll be back in a second, okay?" She started toward the bathroom before he could object. She turned around and saw him paying while he waited.

When they finally entered her dorm, he had her laughing so hard that she grabbed onto his shoulder as she doubled over. She hadn't expected to genuinely enjoy his company, but she wasn't about to complain. How many boring and sometimes downright offensive guys had she taken to bed only because she needed feed? The longer she'd been at college, the ratio of good guys to jerks had gotten worse. It made her appreciate the good ones even more.

He smiled at her and the sexual energy that had been building around her and inside her burst out. He seemed to feel it, too, because he stopped talking and just stared at her like he wanted to eat her alive. She just might let him if it would let her stop thinking for the night. He leaned down and kissed her for the first time and it was if she had stepped on a live wire. She reached up and held his face in her hands, wanting to get closer *immediately*.

When he eventually broke their kiss, he was breathing heavily, and his eyes were dilated. It was always the same reaction with the boys and men she kissed ever since she grew into her powers. She just hoped he wouldn't be too overwhelmed by her Supernatural abilities. Unable to prevent herself, she went up on her tiptoes and nipped his bottom lip, drawing a growl from deep in his chest. Without any warning, he grabbed her legs and lifted them around his waist. She grabbed onto his shoulders just in time before she would have otherwise lost balance.

"Where is your bedroom?"

She pointed, and he began walking. He practically tossed her onto her bed and covered her with his body, his hands roaming almost as much as her own.

Ivy closed her eyes. *This* was what she needed. She would let herself go and worry about everything else tomorrow. Tonight, she would just enjoy.

CHAPTER 10

THE PHONE RANG THREE TIMES BEFORE SHE PICKED up. He just hoped she wouldn't let it go to voicemail like she had been doing for the past few days. She answered. "Hey, sis. What's new with you?"

"What do you mean?"

Was she serious? She'd been so happy lately, he felt like he was constantly on some phantom sugar high that made him feel a longing he'd never felt before. "As if you don't know. The twin link gives me an open door to your emotions, remember?"

"Well, I'm just excited to finally be twenty-one."

"Bullshit. You've never cared about birthdays or being able to drink. You barely do it, anyway." Why was she lying to him?

"Well, maybe I changed my mind. Besides, why does it matter what the reason is? Can't I be happy?"

"Of course, you can. I was just wondering. Don't get mad at me for being curious."

"I'm just happy, Alec. There's nothing else to tell you."

"Uh huh."

"I'm serious. How have you been?"

"Fine. Like you insist on saying, nothing much is happening." Which was sadly true. He'd been particularly bored with college life lately. If he wasn't already a junior, he'd almost consider dropping out. He'd turned to casual hook ups for entertainment, but they weren't as satisfying as they had once been. If they had started boring him before, now they almost repulsed him because he knew none of them could appease the new longing he'd been feeling ever since he and Fawn turned twenty-one. And she clearly wasn't going to tell him what that was about, so he was still frustratingly clueless about what had changed.

"Now, *I* don't believe you."

"That's okay. At least I know I'm telling the *truth*."

She let out a huff of annoyance.

Now you know how it feels. "I'm glad you're happy, Fawn. And whenever you're ready to tell me why, I'm just a phone call away."

"Love you, Alec. Bye."

The call ended and he immediately texted Ivy, hoping she wasn't with his sister: *What's up with Fawn lately? She wouldn't tell me anything when I asked.*

Three dots appeared, indicating she was typing and he stared at his screen, silently willing her to type faster. Obviously, it didn't work.

When her message finally appeared, it read: *Calm down over there, big brother. She's more than fine now. Caleb's good for her.*

Fawn was dating someone? Did that mean his dream could come true now? He typed back: *Who is he?*

He didn't get a reply, and even though he didn't get a read receipt from her, he knew she'd seen his last message and chosen to ignore it. They'd learned to disable that feature in middle school. She may be a pain in his ass, but she told him more than his sister had. The question now was: what did it all mean?

He was about to call the woman who had the answers when her name appeared on his phone first. "Mom? I was just about to call you."

"Have you talked to Fawn lately?"

"Hello to you, too."

"Sorry, Alec. Hi. I trust you've been doing well."

"More or less."

"I'll be coming back to that, but please answer my question."

"Yeah, I just talked to her. She's been really happy lately. Ivy says she's met someone new. Why are you asking? Did you see something?"

"I don't know."

The words sent a chill through him. "What do you mean you don't know? How is that possible? You *always* know."

"I'm still trying to figure that out. On your birthday, Evelyn visited me to warn me that Fawn was in danger. I went to check her future, but it was fuzzy, and I couldn't make out any details. I haven't been able to reach her lately either."

"Apparently, she's been busy with this guy named Caleb. And you know that school always picks up in November. She's probably working on projects and papers left and right. I can tell her to call you."

"No, that's not necessary. I'll call her myself. But before I do, what's going on with you? Are you not happy?"

He sighed. "I don't know. I'm not as happy as I used to be, but I wouldn't necessarily call myself sad or depressed. I just can't seem to be very interested in anything lately."

"I'm sorry to hear that. When did this start?"

"My birthday."

"Hm. And is that when Fawn met this mysterious Caleb?"

So that *did* have something to do with it. "I think so. Why?"

"I believe the twin link is activating something in you that Fawn is currently experiencing."

"Which is what?"

"I'm not certain. Have you been speaking to Ivy lately?"

What was with all the questions? "Yes..."

"That's good, Alec. It's always important to put as much effort, if not more, into the friends you already have as into making new friends." He heard the house phone buzz, indicating his mom's next client had arrived. "I have to go, Alec. But if you need to call me about anything, I'm here."

"Thanks, Mom. Love you. Bye."

He pocketed his phone and decided to head to the gym. Her random last comment and the lack of answers was getting to him, so he might as well be productive in working it off.

"HEY, CAN I ASK YOU SOMETHING?" FAWN WAS standing in their ridiculously small kitchen with a hot mug of tea in her hands.

Ivy looked up. "Sure. What's up?"

Her friend bit her lip and stayed silent for a moment. Fawn sighed. "I don't know what to do about Caleb."

"I'm going to need more than that. What happened?"

"Well, Caleb specifically called our first dinner not a date to make me feel more comfortable, but he said he'd be interested in going on a date with me in the future."

"That sounds good. And you sound excited, so I don't see where the problem is."

"He hasn't brought it up again. And I want to, but I don't want to sound needy. If he wanted to go on a date with me, he'd say it, right?"

Ah, there it was. "Well, you said he qualified your first dinner as a non-date to make you comfortable. Ever think maybe he's waiting to see if you'd be comfortable for an actual date?"

"But he should know that I am."

"Why? It's only been three weeks. Most people don't change their mind so quickly. And besides, it's not like he's a mind-reader."

Fawn smiled. "Well, he just has this way of reading me that I assumed he would have mentioned something by now."

"Or, you know, you could bring it up." She laughed at her friend's panicked expression. "It's not the end of the world. People do it all the time. It's not a big deal."

"No way. And just because you're confident as hell doesn't mean everyone is."

"Fake it 'til you make it." *And sometimes, even after that.*

Fawn gave her a look and she pasted on a smile. "Ready to go?"

"Yep."

They were silent for the short five-minute walk to the large auditorium where their Abnormal Psychology lecture was held. Ivy noticed Caleb walking behind them in the line of students and pulled Fawn slightly to the side near the door.

As he neared them, she spoke in a stage whisper, "Ask him."

He smiled at both of them and Ivy smiled back, her gaze darting to Fawn then going back to him. He seemed to get the message. "Who and what is being asked of me?"

"Nothing," Fawn said so quickly that even the most oblivious person could tell she was lying. Her friend glared at her, but Ivy just shrugged.

Caleb watched the two of them and laughed, seemingly amused. "Now my curiosity is piqued, but I'll give you the benefit of the doubt and not pry." He opened the door for them and gestured for them to go first.

Ivy climbed the stairs to the row she'd taken to since Caleb came into their lives. She could see that Fawn was practically vibrating with energy in her seat, a cloud of pink surrounding her and reaching out toward Caleb. Caleb, too, was surrounded by one, but it seemed to be more tentative than hers. She smiled, Fawn clearly wasn't the only one unsure of how to proceed in the relationship. The red line between them seemed to glow in the center of their overlapping pink clouds. It looked like a Valentine's Day version of the Threads of Life the Fates were rumored to have in Greek mythology.

Ivy had to restrain herself from feeding off it. It had been a growing issue in the past few weeks as the two grew closer and hung out in their suite, practically dangling their affection for each other in front of her. But she had decided a long time ago that she never wanted to feed off her best friend or her brother. And now she was *definitely* keeping to that after what happened with Jackson. She suppressed a shudder. She had been doing a lot better, but he'd still slip into her thoughts every so often.

She decided to focus on her friend again. And the fact that she was clearly not talking to Caleb. She pulled out her phone and shot off a text: *Stop eye-fucking each other and get a room!* There, that should do the trick.

Fawn's eyes read her screen then shot to hers. A blush was spreading on her cheeks and she quickly turned away from Ivy and Caleb.

At the end of class, Ivy was frustrated with her best friend. What was she, Cupid? When Fawn turned to pick her coat off the back of her seat, Ivy met her gaze and mentally shouted at her, *Ask him already!* As her row emptied, she passed Fawn and pointed to Caleb before leaving for the cafeteria to get a good spot in line.

Ivy got her food and sat down at an empty table for two. She was checking her phone for texts when she heard someone sit down. She looked up and saw her hookup from the night before across from her. "Erik, what are you doing here?"

He didn't answer and stared at her with a love-struck gaze that made her stomach clench in anxiety. Was he another Jackson? She'd been more careful lately to keep ahead of her cravings like her mom suggested. Had she inadvertently pumped him for more energy?

Her worrying was interrupted when Fawn and Caleb came to stand next to the table. She stood up and hugged Fawn, needing the comfort more than she expected.

"I didn't realize we weren't meeting alone," her friend whispered.

"Oh, I can send him away." The myths about sirens being able to manipulate men to their will was not exaggerated. Just misguided in the *method*. They didn't sing to hypnotize men. Men simply became addicted to them. "He's just a hookup from last night."

"Yes, I remember you two coming in."

Ivy blushed. She always tried to be quiet the few times she hooked up in her own dorm room, but apparently, she failed last night. Ivy turned back to the guy in question. "My friend and I need some girl time. Could you give us some privacy? I'll text you later." He was good in bed. What was the harm in having another night with him?

He stood up and left them without a word.

She saw Fawn staring at her incredulously. "He's not really one for words." Okay, time for a subject change before too many questions were asked. Caleb had a knowing look in his eye that made her nervous. Was he a Hunter? She quickly dismissed the thought. His posture was wrong. He wasn't militaristic enough to be one of them. "I see you also brought a surprise plus one."

Fawn turned to Caleb, who stepped forward. "Just wanted to say hello and let you know Fawn and I will be going on a date tonight. I understand good friends such as you like to be kept apprised of such social arrangements."

She trained her eyes on Fawn. "Really? This is the first time I've heard of it." She hoped her eyes conveyed her question: *Why didn't you text me?*

"We *just* made the plan."

"Uh huh. I want details. Now."

Caleb cleared his throat. "I'll see you tonight, then." He hugged Fawn and left.

When he was gone, Ivy turned back to Fawn. "Spill."

"Can I get something to eat first?"

"Dish now, food later."

Fawn rolled her eyes. "Well, I took your advice and finally asked if he wanted to go out with me and he said yes."

"I knew he would. He'd be an idiot to turn you down." And in denial, given how attracted he was to her.

"Can I finish?"

She waved her on. "Proceed."

"I'm going over to his apartment after our tutoring session. And he's going to make me dinner before we watch a movie."

A little traditional, but given how Caleb sometimes talked, that wasn't exactly surprising. "That sounds amazing. You're going to have such a great time." She couldn't resist needling Fawn. "And let's be real, movie-time is just code for second base."

"He has to get past first before I can even consider something beyond that. Anyway, I wanted to ask for your advice because I have no idea what to wear tonight."

"Of course, I'll help you, silly! Now, let's get something to eat. I'm starving over here."

Once they had their food, Fawn asked the other question on her mind. "Am I wrong to be going out with him?"

"What do you mean?"

"Well, he is my tutor. Am I letting him take advantage of me?"

Ivy shook her head. "I don't think so. You're both consenting adults. If you both like each other, I wouldn't worry. But just because you want a relationship now, doesn't mean you can't change your mind."

That night, Ivy felt a twinge of jealousy when Caleb's cloud of pink had turned a darker and deeper shade of magenta as he took in the sight of Fawn. She wanted someone to look at her like that. And not just because she was a siren. Her soulmate would, but that wasn't possible.

CHAPTER 11

ALEC WOKE UP WITH THE IMMEDIATE SENSE THAT something was off. It wasn't something he could immediately name, but it was definitely there. He sat up in bed and went to the bathroom. He flipped on the light and looked in the mirror. He looked the same and his necklace was room temperature. So, what *was* it?

He went about his normal routine and to his classes. It wasn't until it was evening did he realize what had been bothering him all day. He had barely felt Fawn through the twin bond all day. He somehow knew it was still *there*, but it left him feeling incomplete. It made him regret any of the times he had wished he didn't have the magical connection to his sister.

What could have possibly happened to make it dim?

He pulled out his phone and texted Ivy. Fawn hadn't answered any of his previous texts since their last phone call and he needed an answer.

Is everything okay with my sister? She hasn't been responding to my texts.

She's been busy.

Not the most detailed answer he'd been hoping for, but it told him what he needed to know. Well, as much as he could possibly expect Ivy to know about. It's not like *she* could read minds, even if she always seemed to know what was on his mind. He typed back, *Thanks.*

He called his mom. "Hey. Have you been able to see Fawn's future? I woke up feeling like someone turned the volume almost all the way down on our twin bond."

Silence met his revelation.

"Mom? Are you still there?"

"Yes. I don't know what to say, exactly. If you still feel it, my first guess is that perhaps she's learned to mentally shield herself. I'm still trying to figure out what's happening with her."

How? The last he knew, Fawn wasn't doing any magic. "If she's learning magic, can you teach me, Mom?"

"Yes, absolutely. I think that's a good idea. I'll get back to you about a curriculum and schedule. In the meantime, stay alert and keep tabs on Fawn until I can find a way to see her future again."

"Will do, Mom. Love you. Bye."

W HEN IVY OPENED HER FRIEND'S DOOR TO BORROW her curling wand because hers had decided to suddenly stop working, the last thing she expected to see was Fawn and Caleb sitting on the floor with their heads close enough to be kissing.

Ivy smiled. "Sorry, didn't know you had company. I'll be out of your hair soon. I just need to get ready to see Erik."

"The guy you were with yesterday at lunch?"

She nodded and walked into the bathroom. Was she making a mistake with seeing Erik again? She shook her head. Too late to cancel now. She set down the iron, unplugged it, and ran her fingers through her hair to loosen the newly-formed coils, bringing it closer to her natural wavy nature. God, why was she trying so hard?

She left the bathroom, grabbed her coat and purse, and went to meet Erik at his dorm.

He opened the door. "You look amazing."

She shrugged out of her coat and walked into his room. "Thank you." She sat down on the foot of his bed.

He kissed her. She lost herself to the sensation, allowing herself to revel in his energy even as her mind wandered.

He wrapped his arm around her waist, pulling her back to him. "Ivy, I'm so glad you agreed to see me again."

She turned and smiled at him. "Erik..." How did she tell him this was the end for them? "I've had a great time with you, but—"

He cut her off. "But this is the end."

She nodded.

He sighed. "I knew it. I just didn't want to believe it."

"I'm sorry."

He let out a humorless laugh. "Don't be. My friends told me it was coming. I can't say I'm surprised. I just hoped it'd be different for us." He paused, just staring at her. "Bye, Ivy. You're one hell of a woman. I'm glad I got to know you, even if it was for such a short time."

When Ivy got back to her dorm, she wanted nothing more than to shower, but her best friend had other ideas.

Fawn sat her down on the couch and asked, "You've always been good at reading guys... Could you tell me what Caleb thinks about me?"

"He's definitely attracted to you. But he's confused about it too. Maybe just give him some time to think it all through."

"Are you sure?"

"Yes."

"How?"

Ivy sighed. "Because... I just know." It was clear in her eyes even without her powers. Why wasn't it to Fawn?

"But how?"

All the questions were bound to happen at some point, but that didn't mean she wanted to deal with them now. It seemed she didn't have a choice anymore. "It's one of a siren's powers."

"A siren?"

"We can sense love and lust. It's how we find prey."

"We? You're one of them?"

She couldn't help but flinch. To hear such alienating words from her best friend unsettled her more than she ever thought it could.

"I'm sorry, Ivy. You know I didn't mean it like that. I'm just a little surprised here. How long have you been keeping this from me?"

"Since forever? But before you get super mad, I didn't actually grow into my abilities until puberty. It's one of the reasons I hid it from you earlier and why I always have a date. Men literally can't resist me." She tried to smile, but it probably looked as fake as it felt.

Fawn sat back as she absorbed everything. "I have a siren for a best friend... It's like I'm living in a paranormal romance novel."

She sighed. "I still fantasize about getting it on with a werewolf. Can you imagine how savage they must be when they finally—"

Fawn slapped her hands over her ears. "Stop it, Ivy! Don't corrupt me any more than you already have. I beg you."

Ivy laughed. *That* was what her friend drew the line at? God love Fawn, but she was so naïve sometimes. "We're in college now. It's natural for people to sleep together."

"You said 'prey'... you don't lure people to their deaths, do you?"

"No, of course not! Sirens thrive off sexual energy and it's kind of addicting, so the more we have of it, the more we need. No one is hurt in the process."

"Isn't that what succubae do?"

She rolled her eyes. "Succubae don't exist."

Her friend frowned. "What do you mean?"

"Remember how supposedly Hathor and Isis were originally one goddess, but the Egyptians worried she was too powerful, so they split her in two? People don't want to think sirens can hunt out of water, so they created the idea of succubae, but they never really existed." She sighed. *Men* being threatened by women's power. Such an old story that never, unfortunately, seemed to go out of fashion.

"Caleb knew about you instantly."

That got her attention. "Really?"

"He's an angel, that's how he knew. He's my guardian angel. He told me someone close to me was keeping a secret, but I never guessed it'd be you. Why didn't you ever tell me? You knew about my magic."

Ivy squashed the guilt she felt rising before it could fully engulf her. "I would have told you if I could, but my mom forbade me because if the word got out, it could make us a target to Hunters."

"Hunters?"

Clearly no one had ever warned her friend. But why wouldn't Stella have told her daughter? Then again, she hadn't told either Fawn or Alec about their magical heritage until the night they received their magic. "Paranormally gifted humans who are dedicated to the extermination of the Supernatural. It's pretty hypocritical if you ask me."

"How horrible."

"My family was attacked by them a few decades ago. That's why my mom moved us to America." She said the words quickly, so she wouldn't dwell and then cry. That hadn't done her any good when it happened, or any time after.

"I never would've guessed."

"That was kind of the point."

Fawn hugged her. "I promise to keep your secret."

"Thank you."

"You sound surprised," Fawn said. "Did you really doubt that I wouldn't share your nature with other people?"

"No, of course not." She paused before admitting, "Well, I thought you might at least tell Alec..."

"If you don't want me to, I won't say a word."

Ivy pulled her into another hug. She paused before adding, "Okay, let's move onto something happier. Pizza and movie night?"

Fawn laughed. "I don't see why not."

Ivy pulled up the app and ordered their regular pizza while Fawn picked the movie. Twenty minutes later, her phone buzzed telling her their food was there. "Pause it for me?" Her friend did it immediately and she went down to meet the delivery guy at the door.

He was cute. Blond hair and couldn't have been older than twenty-three. She could tell he was fit, too, even through the sweater.

He looked her up and down. "You look nice." He held out the box.

She took it from him, feeling a small piece of paper underneath it. "Thank you."

When she got back up to her room, she couldn't help but smile.

Fawn saw her and said, "Was he cute?"

"Yes. Gave me his number, too." She put the box down and grabbed two plates from the kitchen.

"Are you going to call him?"

She couldn't even think about that right now. All she could think about was how lucky to have such a good friend as Fawn, who accepted her nature. She wondered if Alec would be as accepting.

CHAPTER 12

"ARE YOU THERE?" HIS SISTER'S VOICE WAS THREADBARE, and he desperately wished he could hug her.

Alec shook himself out of his shocked stupor. "Yes. I'm here. Tell me again what happened."

"I—I was attacked by demons."

"What? When? Where? How did you get away? How did you survive? Are you okay?"

"I used magic."

So, she *was* learning magic? "But how did you learn to do that?"

"It just came to me. I didn't even cast a specific spell."

He suspected she was lying. "Who were they?"

"They're Black-Eyed Beings. They looked human at first, but when I set one on fire, they were covered in black scales."

"How do you know that? More importantly, how did they find you?"

"I just wanted to tell you what happened and that I'm okay," she said. "Alec, I'm really tired. I'm going to rest for a bit."

"Okay. Take care of yourself." He hung up and stared at the screen. How had he not known about the attack? The question was, with his mom still unable to predict Fawn's future, what would happen next?

"STAY STILL, FAWN!" IVY ADMONISHED HER FRIEND. My God, one would think that her friend was allergic to the idea of primping.

"How much longer are you going to take? You've been working on my hair for twenty minutes."

"That is because your hair *refuses* to hold any shape. It's too silky for the pins to grip on their own." Ivy placed in the final bobby pin, pushing it as far into the center as it would go, and grabbed the hairspray again. "Close your eyes and cover your face." Then she started spraying again.

"Oh, is that why you're using enough hairspray to gas a large army of insects?"

"Stop complaining. I'm done. Look." She'd put Fawn's hair into an intricate bun. She was pretty proud of it, if she was honest. Ivy had spent the past hour curling each individual, one-inch strand, and then twisting and tucking with the help of a whole pack of bobby pins and, as Fawn rightly assessed, a lot of hairspray. Half a can, to be precise.

"It's beautiful." Her friend started to stand up.

She placed a hand on her shoulder. "Where are you going? I'm not done with you."

"But you just said—"

"I meant with your *hair*. Now it's time for makeup."

"God, Ivy—"

"I was thinking dark colors to match your..."

"I'm not letting you go all operatic on me. It's a dance, Ivy, not a theater production."

"Give me more credit here."

"Natural colors, Ivy. Or I do my own makeup."

"Fine, but you have to let me do purple smoky eyes. It emphasizes your blue eyes."

Fawn rolled her eyes then tilted her head up. "Go ahead."

"Thank you." Ivy grabbed her eyeshadow palette and got to work. When she was done, she pushed Fawn toward the mirror.

"Oh my God. I look almost as amazing as you. And like Tinkerbell used all her pixie dust on me to make it happen."

"You sell yourself short. It's all you. I just helped. Anyway, go put your dress on. I'll meet you and Caleb in a bit."

Fawn smiled and went into her bedroom. Ivy checked the mirror to make sure her own makeup hadn't smudged in the process and was glad to see it looked as fresh as when she'd first applied it. Now, all she had to do was put on her dress.

She pulled it out of the closet and admired it. Ironic as it may be, she'd gone for the mermaid look. Two weeks ago, she'd bought an iridescent bluish-green dress with a ruched bodice and tight skirt that hugged her curves and was guaranteed to make every boy in the room go crazy with desire. She stepped into her teal heels first, then the dress, reaching behind her and zipping it up to her waist. She went to the jewelry box on her dresser and removed the iridescent mask that resembled mother of pearl.

She tied the black ribbon around the back of her head and grabbed her purse. When she walked out to their entry way, she found Fawn and Caleb standing together. The sight made her both thrilled for her best friend and sadly jealous that she didn't have the same happiness. Would Alec even look at her like Caleb did with Fawn if he could see her now? She shook her head. It didn't matter anymore. She'd draw enough attention tonight to ignore it.

A LEC SAT CROSS-LEGGED ON HIS DORM ROOM FLOOR and listened to his mom speak on the phone. They'd been on the phone for twenty minutes and he had just about had it. "Why do I have to do this? I asked you to teach me magic. Not turn me into a hippie."

"Meditating is an important part of focus, which is the foundation of all magic. Remember what happened with your sister."

How could he forget? Fawn had set her room on fire by accident because she focused on creating fire, not lighting the candles she had meant to. It was enough to scare her off magic ever since. Well, until she secretly began learning magic this year.

"Now, take another deep breath and clear your mind."

Like he ever could. He had to learn magic, so he could help his sister. Who knew how long she'd be safe? He bet demons didn't attack just anyone, and the way his mom had reacted when he told her the news, it didn't appear like it would be a one-time thing.

He sighed and closed his eyes. He waited for a few moments and was surprised to find that this time his mind emptied. Third time's the charm, apparently. "Okay. Now what?"

"I want you to visualize a protective shield surrounding you. Picture what it looks like. What does it feel like? Is it flexible or rigid? How far does it reach?"

Alec followed his mother's voice and pictured an invisible shield modeled after the ones he'd seen in the movie adaptations of some of his sister's favorite books. Those had pulsed with power and protected their caster's well. Well, at least one had. The other was broken by a large group of attackers. He hoped that his twin magic and Fawn's supercharged powers would be enough to prevent that from happening if it ever came down to it.

He opened his eyes and saw that he'd done it. "I did it!" His excitement caused the shield to evaporate into the air as if it had never been there, and he felt his confidence deflate. "It's gone."

"That's good, Alec. Eventually, you'll learn to maintain it even while focusing on other things and even using other magic."

He heard her but was already busy willing the shield back into existence—this time with his eyes open. It appeared within seconds and pulsed with each breath. When he was confident it wouldn't go away, he asked, "How long will that take?"

He heard his mother sigh. "It's hard to say, Alec. It all takes practice. And time."

He rolled his eyes. He saw that answer coming. This time, he intentionally dispersed the protective shield. He'd definitely be practicing that later. But he needed more skills in his arsenal. "What else can I learn now?"

IVY NOTICED HIM ON THE OTHER SIDE OF the bar. Well, technically, he had noticed her first, but she caught him staring. She smiled at him. He pointed to the bartender and she turned to see that he was bringing her a red drink she hadn't ordered.

"Compliments of the guy over there," the bartender said.

"Thanks," she said, eyeing the drink. God, she wished she could tell whether it was safe. Unfortunately, being a siren didn't protect her from all the modern dangers of being a woman. Even though people were especially attracted to her and fell under her thrall, if someone *did* try to drug her, it still wouldn't end well.

She'd cut out of the Halloween party the same time Fawn and Caleb had and had been fending off advances since. Normally, she wouldn't have cared. It was a regular occurrence but spending the evening with her best friend and her soulmate made a meaningless hookup less appealing. Which wasn't great given she found herself craving more energy than she had in a while.

The guy in question took the seat next to her. This close, she noticed there was something decidedly Supernatural about him. His flawless skin and predatory smile made a chill ran down her spine once she realized what he was. The man standing before her was a vampire. She sat straighter in her seat.

"Hello, little siren."

"Hello," she said. Was she supposed to call him "sir," or something? She'd never actually met a vampire before. She cursed herself for not noticing what he was earlier.

There wasn't a rule that sirens couldn't mingle with other Supernaturals, but without any defensive powers of their own, it was often more dangerous than feeding from a regular human. Ivy didn't believe for a second her Krav Maga training would stand a chance against vampire speed.

"I noticed no one has caught your eye tonight."

"I would say I agree, but then I'd be lying."

"Who's the lucky girl?"

He smiled. It wasn't quite menacing, but danger lingered underneath the gleaming row of white teeth. "Can't you guess?"

She nodded.

He took the drink he'd bought her and held it up to her lips. "It's not poisoned," he said. "I'm not in the habit of drugging my partners for the night." He caressed her cheek with the back of his other hand and she struggled not to flinch from his cold touch. "Ruins the taste."

"Who says you'll be getting a taste of me at all?"

He leaned forward, and she saw his eyes darken. Unlike human irises, his seemed to swirl in a hypnotic pattern that she would easily bet entranced human prey. "Because I think you and I are looking for the same thing."

She took a deep breath to steady herself. "How do you figure?"

"Neither of us are looking for anything permanent, and we're both bored with the human variety. Why not indulge in something more interesting for a change?" He licked his lips. "I've never had a siren as young as you."

Damn it, he made a good point. She could feel the sexual energy rolling off him in waves and it was at least five times as potent as any human she'd ever hooked up with. And they hadn't done anything but *talk* to each other.

"Is there any chance you secretly made this a legitimate Bloody Mary?" She watched for his reaction.

"None at all."

"And you expect me to believe that?"

He smiled, his fangs briefly flashing before disappearing again.

"What guarantee do I have that I'll get out alive? And I do mean that literally. I have no plans to become a vampire tonight."

"You have my solemn oath that you will emerge the same siren as you are now. I'm not in the siring business. Like I said, I'm not interested in anything permanent. Besides, I wouldn't want to kill you, even with my blood in your system, and the guarantee of you becoming immortal. I much prefer you with warm blood running through your veins."

Ivy took a sip of the drink and let the fire burn down her throat. She wasn't going to get any more reassurances than what he'd already given her. She just hoped he hadn't lied. "Let's get out of here."

He took her hand, making her pause. "I live upstairs. Perk of owning the bar."

"Sneaky."

He shrugged. "You're not going to back out, are you?"

"No." She couldn't afford to *not* feed tonight. She didn't want another incident like Jackson.

He led her to the back and together they climbed the stairs to his loft apartment, decked out in dark curtains.

He took off her coat and began kissing her. When he moved to her neck, she tensed, but he continued down to her shoulder. She found herself relaxing into it. *This* she could do. It was just physical after all. So, why did she feel like she was somehow cheating on Alec?

As if sensing her internal conflict, the vampire raised his head. "You're thinking an awful lot."

"Not used to a brain in your conquests?"

He smiled, his fangs now on full display. "On the contrary. But many of my lovers prefer that I *help* them let go. I can do the same for you. All you have to do is say the word, little siren."

Before she could think twice, she said, "Please." It was the closest she had ever come to actually begging. She needed to stop thinking about Alec, and nothing else had seemed to work tonight.

Ivy gasped in pain when his fangs broke her skin, then moaned in pleasure as he began to drink. Moments later, she felt the fangs retract and felt his tongue against her skin, healing the puncture marks. She barely heard the vampire murmur, "Just as sweet as I hoped."

Between his bite and his overwhelming sexual energy, she launched into a light-headed euphoria. She gripped his shoulders tightly, grounding herself in reality as her mind floated off.

CHAPTER 13

Alec didn't know what was happening. One moment, he was sleeping in his dorm, and the next, he was being chased in all-consuming darkness by a group of people. He turned and saw the recognizable faces of girls he'd shared classes with over the years. All of whom he'd slept with at one point or another. Fear seized his heart, making him run faster. They caught up to him, their hands grabbing him and pulling him down. He looked at the hand gripping his arm and realized it wasn't human. It was black and covered in scales. Black-Eyed Beings. How had they found *him*? And hadn't Fawn said she defeated them?

It's just a nightmare, he told himself. *Just* wake up *and everything will be fine!* That seemed to break him free of the dream, but looking around, he couldn't recognize where he was. It definitely wasn't his college dorm. It looked like he was in a giant throne room, but it was so dark, save a few bonfires.

"Ah, look who's finally awake."

Alec turned his head and saw a man in a black suit. He'd never seen him before, but a sense of foreboding raced down his spine and goosebumps peppered his skin as if he were chilled from the inside out. "Who are you?"

The stranger smiled. "Where are my manners? I'm Lucifer. I'm sure you've heard of me. It's nice to meet you."

"What the hell?"

He made a sweeping bow. "Welcome to my humble abode."

"Wait, I'm *in* Hell?" That couldn't be possible. Was it? He looked down and noticed that his feet weren't touching the ground. He seemed to be floating, paralyzed except for his head.

"You're not here to stay. I just needed you to get your sister's attention." Lucifer twisted his hand and Alec found himself pivoting in the air. Now, Alec could see two black iron thrones each with a fire gem embedded in the top seated among piles of bones.

It didn't take an idiot to figure out who the second throne was for.

Alec glared at the Devil. "I'd tell you to rot in Hell, but it seems you already are."

The man dropped his smile and took a measured step forward. Before he could do anything else, someone spoke up.

"Alec." He recognized his mom's voice and froze all over again. If they were both in Hell, things had gone horribly wrong. Her next words were weak, "Contact Fawn."

His eyes darted to the Devil, who said, "Listen to your mother."

"How do I do that?"

Lucifer made a *tsk*-ing sound. "You haven't even taught him the basics yet, Ms. Belgrave? I'm disappointed in you."

He could hear the venom in his mother's voice even as she instructed him, "Close your eyes and focus only on your twin bond and reaching your sister. Tell her where we are."

He hesitated, and Lucifer said, "Well, go on already."

He looked to his mom, who nodded. Well, he never thought he'd be doing the Devil's bidding. Definitely not with his mother's blessing.

He closed his eyes and focused on doing what his mother said. "We've been kidnapped. Be careful."

"Something evil is brewing," Stella added.

Lucifer began clapping, breaking Alec's concentration. Alec opened his eyes and glared at the man who had literally made his life a living Hell.

"Well done, both of you," Lucifer continued. Behind him, two giant double doors opened and a young man with black wings flew into the room. "Perfect timing. Caleb, I'd like you to meet Fawn's family."

The new arrival came to a full stop and stared up at him and his mom, a guilty look on his face.

Caleb? He recognized that name. *This* was the guy Fawn had been dating? And he worked for the Devil? What had Ivy been thinking?

"And now," Lucifer said to both of them, "if you'll excuse me, I'm off to collect my grand prize. You'll both be home in no time. Thank you for your cooperation. Caleb, are you coming? I'm sure Fawn will be needing you soon."

Caleb gave them one last look before he turned and followed the Devil back out of the doors.

A moment passed before Alec could move again. He turned to his mom who looked just as surprised as he. Before he could ask her what they should do, he felt himself being propelled upward, then like he was free-falling through the sky. He opened his eyes and was back in bed. Taking in the blue walls, he realized he wasn't at school, but in his *childhood* room. In New York City.

He pulled out his phone and dialed Ivy. "Pick up, pick up, pick up, pick up." When she finally did, he said, "Ivy, how could you do this?"

"What are you talking about, Alec?" She sounded groggy.

"Guess what I just found out."

"Can't this wait until tomorrow?"

"No, Ivy. It can't. Because I just found out that Caleb has been working for the Devil the whole time."

"Wh—what? How do you know that?"

"I just saw him during my trip to Hell. My mom was there, too. She's unharmed, in case you were worried."

IVY CLUTCHED HER PHONE TO HER EAR. She couldn't believe what she was hearing. How could she have been so wrong about Caleb?

"Alec, I had no idea—"

"Weirdly enough, I was able to figure that part out for myself."

That pissed her off. "It's not *all* my fault, you know. Fawn has magic, and so do you. And your mom didn't see anything." What was she saying? Playing the blame game wasn't what she wanted to do. "Alec, that's not what I meant."

"Of course not."

She winced at his sharp tone. "I'm sorry, Alec."

"I don't want to talk to you about this. Have a good night, Ivy." He hung up and she stared at the blank screen. What had she done? Oh, God. She had to call Fawn.

She dialed her and went straight to voice mail. "No, no, no, no." What if something had gone horribly wrong?

Her hookup from that night touched her arm. "Hey, are you okay?"

She turned around. "No. My friend is in trouble. I have to go."

"Right now?"

She kissed him on the cheek. "Yes, right now." She got dressed faster than she ever had before and got back to the dorm half an hour later. To her horror, it was empty. *Shit.*

She checked the clock. It was only five in the morning. She went to the café. Caffeine was the only way she'd be able to function for the rest of the day. She had just sat down with her order when she saw him coming. She stood and braced herself when he walked up to her table.

"You can relax. I just want to talk to you."

Ivy crossed her arms and sent him a look. "Just like you love my friend, but still betrayed her? Yeah, I don't think I'll be relaxing any time soon." His expression became one of surprise, and she rolled her eyes. "Alec told me everything once he and Stella made touchdown on Earth again after being abducted by the freaking Devil, who I now know is your boss."

"Not anymore," Caleb snapped. He took a deep breath. "I understand you're angry with me for hurting Fawn, but I need you to listen."

"Why should I? Do you know how much I've had to deal with? I had to tell my best friend's family I didn't pick up on your shady character—much to my shame—and I don't know how to help my best friend. I looked like an idiot because of you! And Alec blames me—as he should. You don't know how much I hated being on the other end when he told me what happened." She let out a frustrated cry. "This is all *your* fault!"

He didn't defend himself, which only upset her more.

"Speaking of her family, do you think you could call them for me? I need them to hear what I have to say."

"Why would I ever agree to do something to help you out? If I haven't already made myself *abundantly* clear I don't like you. And I'd go as far to say 'I hate you,' and I don't use that word lightly, asshole."

"Could you give me a break, Ivy? I'm here trying to make amends with your best friend and maybe even try to save her from Hell." He paused. "Fawn is hurt because I was stupid—"

"Isn't that the truth?"

"I thought you were going to let me make my case."

He had nerve. "Those words never left my mouth, pretty boy."

He sighed. "Fawn is suffering because of the soulmate bond."

Ivy closed the distance between them and glared up at him. God, if only murder wasn't a capital crime. "Say that again." He started to, but she interrupted him. "Swear on your mother's grave and look me in the eye as you repeat yourself. You better not lie to me. You can't play around with something as serious as soulmates."

He sighed and met her gaze straight on. "I swear on my mother's grave that Fawn Belgrave is my soulmate and in pain because she is denying our connection."

Ivy took a step back and whispered, "Shit." This was bad on so many levels. Her mom had warned her about what happened when soulmates weren't together. She was starting to know how *that* felt, and it sucked.

"Will you do this for Fawn?"

How dare he even ask that? "I'd do anything for her and her family. She's practically my sister."

Caleb nodded in thanks.

He seemed to think that was the end of the conversation. He was wrong. "Which means," Ivy continued, putting as much steel into her voice as she could. "if you hurt her again, I will hunt you down and castrate you."

He had the good sense to back away from her. "I understand. She's lucky to have you as a friend."

She stared him down for a few more moments before nodding and picking up her phone. It barely rang once before Alec picked up. "Ivy! Tell me you found some insight into how we can help Fawn." Clearly, he'd decided he needed her again. Not that she'd bring it up.

"Calm down. I do have news, but I don't know how much you'll like it." She paused. "Caleb is asking to speak to you and Stella."

"The asshole is with you?" She could practically feel his anger through the small device. It made her glad he wasn't there to strangle Fawn's soulmate. She still couldn't believe that.

Caleb grabbed the phone from her. "I apologize for my past actions. Truly, I am sorry."

There was a pause. Then Caleb began repeating his explanation. Before he could finish, Ivy took the phone from him again and said, "I don't completely trust Caleb, but when he and Fawn were together, I always saw a true bond of affection. He seemed to change the longer they were together. Despite his betrayal, he was—and is—genuinely in love with Fawn. I don't think he's lying to us now. I made him swear on his dead mother's grave when he told me."

"I see," Stella's quiet voice shouldn't have surprised her, but it did. How long had she been listening?

Before she could ask, Caleb took the phone back. This time, she let him. He repeated his question, "Will you help me, Stella? Alec?"

"Of course, we will," Alec grumbled. "I don't like you, but I'll help save my sister."

Stella agreed, and Ivy prayed that she was on the way to being forgiven by the Belgraves.

CHAPTER 14

ALEC STARED AT THE PHONE AND REMINDED HIMSELF that it wasn't ready for an upgrade for another two months. Because he wanted to smash it into a million pieces.

His sister was being hunted by the actual Devil, and now he was supposed to believe that such a silly thing as soulmates existed? What had his life come to?

He turned to his mom. "I can't believe you agreed to help him. It's *his* fault that she's in Hell to begin with."

"He was being controlled by Lucifer, Alec."

"He could have disobeyed."

"But he didn't—"

"That's my point."

"Alec, it happened. But he *is* your sister's soulmate—"

He scoffed at that.

"And he wants to help her now," his mom continued. "And he knows more about Hell than I do. We need him if we're going to save Fawn. And she'll need him, too."

"Why on *Earth* would she need him?"

"Because he's her soulmate."

"You keep saying that, and not only is the existence of soulmates ridiculous, him being *hers* is crazy. If soulmates were real, he shouldn't be hurting her this way."

His mother smiled at him. It wasn't her usual happy smile. Or even the one that she gave when she was annoyed but covering it up. This was the one that she always gave right before teaching him or Fawn a lesson in life.

"Not now, Mom. We don't have time for you to lecture me."

"You need to hear this."

"I don't have to like Caleb to work with him. I just needed someone to complain to."

He stood up and she touched his arm. "Sit, Alec." He did. "I never told you this, but our family has a history of complicated relationships with soulmates. Even the good ones."

"I know that, but this is more than a few arguments mixed in with years of knowing that you love someone, Mom."

"It is," she agreed. "But what I'm saying is, no relationship is perfect. And, like anything worthwhile, soulmate relationships require hard work and dedication to achieve and maintain."

"It's not the same, Mom. He lied about who he was to spy on Fawn for the Devil. That's unforgivable."

"Perhaps, but your forgiveness is not the one he really needs. And you must also remember, he was teaching Fawn magic which, if what you told me about the Black-Eyed Beings attack was true, likely saved your sister's life."

Why did his Mom always have to be right? "Okay, forgetting all that. I need to learn magic. For real this time. Just meditating didn't help before and now that we *know* there are things out there after Fawn, I need to know how to protect her."

She stood up. "Come into the Reading room."

He followed her. He'd never spent much time behind the dark mahogany door that led into the mystical sanctuary. She pulled on a gold rope hanging from the ceiling and the embroidered dark purple curtain before him moved aside to reveal a medium-sized ebony table.

He sat and tapped his hands on the surface and watched his mother gather a few things from the cabinet in the corner. She unrolled a velvet purple mat and placed a small, silvery pouch on it. She tugged on the small ribbon and removed a deck of large cards with a brown and yellow lattice background with a multicolored cross decorated with symbols and what looked like multiple wheels of petals, each with their own Hebrew letter. He recognized some of the individual characters, but now he wished he hadn't dropped out of Hebrew school. Maybe he'd be able to read it if he hadn't.

"You're going to give me a Reading? I thought you were going to teach me some defensive magic."

"Not yet. I gave Fawn a Reading, and despite not being able to see her future with full clarity, the cards haven't been wrong yet."

"What did she get?"

His mother waved him off and handed him the deck. "Shuffle and stop when you're ready. Then pick four cards and place them face-down here, here, here, and here." She gestured three spots in a line on the fabric, then one above.

He shuffled, trying hard not to bend the cards that his mom had used for so many years and continued to do so for her job on a daily basis. When he was done, he laid out the cards as instructed and handed the deck back to her. "Now what?" He'd never seen his mom do a Reading. Fawn had when they were younger, but he hadn't cared.

She flipped the first card he'd put down. He leaned closer and saw the image of a man on a chariot pulled by a bull, holding a scepter in his right hand and a geometric globe in his left. At the bottom of monochrome art-deco style frame, he read, "Prince of Disks."

"That's your past." She looked up at him. "It means new advice will help you achieve your goals." She flipped the next card.

He took in the depressing image of what looked like a collapsing house being engulfed in flames beneath a shining eye in the sky, abstract people jumping from the roof, a dove in the top left corner and what looked like a haloed snake. In the top of the same frame as the previous card, there was the roman numeral for sixteen, and at the bottom, it read, "The Tower."

"That doesn't look promising," he said.

"It's not as morbid as it looks," his mom promised. "But it does mean sudden change, often caused by traumatic events. And it usually indicates that a threat is present."

"No kidding." He'd definitely classify Lucifer being after Fawn as a current threat.

"Relationships also play a pivotal role when this card appears."

Immediately, Ivy came to mind, but he pushed the thought away.

"Now, the Future card." His mother flipped the next card and he sucked in a breath, his gaze drawn immediately to the bottom after seeing the skeleton and scythe. "Death? Am I going to die? Is Fawn?"

His mother shook her head. "It's another card indicating change. It's painful, but not necessarily a bad thing."

He looked closer at the image and noticed that there seemed to be a spirit behind the black skeleton and a blue scorpion at the bottom. The roman number thirteen was on the top of the frame and he let out a humorless laugh. An unlucky number for a scary card. Not surprising at all.

Unable to deal with the suspense, he flipped over the last card himself. It was the most colorful of all the ones he picked. He saw a white lion and red bird sitting on fire and hunched over a giant gold pot with the small image of a raven on a skull on the front. The two animals made him think of fire and ice. But it was the rest of the image that had his attention: A two-headed woman, one with a blue head, the other with white had the opposite color arm on their side of an invisible, dividing line that made them mirror images of each other. Well, almost reflections. Besides the coloring, the blue hand held what looked like fire or some of Zeus' legendary lightning bolts and the white hand was pouring a white liquid from a blue cup. The number fourteen was on top and the bottom read, "Temperance."

"If the last three cards were my past, present, and future, what's this? You already explained all of those."

"This is the Outcome card. But you seemed to look at this one a lot. What does it say to you?"

"Fire and ice. Opposites."

His mother nodded. "You're on the right track. It's actually about balance and harmony. It's an optimistic card, too."

"That explains all the colors." He pushed back from his seat. "Okay, now that you've given me a Reading, *now* can I learn some magic?"

His mother nodded, then meticulously put away the deck and mat. He waited impatiently for her in the living room. When she came out, she had a book with her that resembled the Grimoire he'd seen on his sixteenth birthday, but it was smaller. She sat next to him on the couch and said, "Let's begin."

Ivy opened the door and glared at the uninvited visitor. She debated on ignoring him, but knowing him, he would have stayed out there all day. "What are *you* doing here?" A frantic month had passed where Ivy spent every spare moment on the phone with Alec or Stella, asking what she could do. The answer was always the same. "Nothing."

The good news was Fawn had magically returned on her own. Although she knew Caleb had something to do with it because he sounded distraught during his last phone call with all of them *after* Fawn had returned. He'd told them he'd gone to Hell to free her, but that it was God who had gotten her out on a technicality.

But this was the first time he had come by in person since their talk in the coffee shop the day Fawn had been taken.

"Can I come in?"

"Can fish climb trees?"

"I'll take that as a 'no,' then." He put his hands into his jean pockets, making him look smaller than she'd ever seen him. Being apart from Fawn was clearly taking a toll on him, too.

Dammit, why had she noticed that? Now she felt bad. "Why do you want to come in?"

"I just want to talk to her."

"She won't want to talk to you."

"That's okay. I just came to apologize and explain why I did what I did."

"I don't know if that's incredibly brave or stupid."

"There's more. She's in danger. Will you let me in?"

She sighed. If this back-fired, Alec would likely kill her. "Yes, but if she tells you to leave, I can't help you." She turned, giving him enough space to enter. "Stay out here. I'll go tell Fawn."

In Fawn's bedroom, she found her friend busy moving around as if someone had hit fast-forward on life. Ivy saw a large trash bag at the bottom of the bed. When Fawn had returned after a month of being in Hell, she had decided to purge her room. Ivy still wasn't sure if it was a good idea, but it had distracted Fawn, so it wasn't an awful one.

Apparently, she waited too long to talk because Fawn stopped moving and turned to her. "What's wrong?"

Damn, she hadn't come up with a way to say this. She looked down at her hands, interlinking her fingers, then unlinking them, willing her mind to give her an eloquent way to break the news. When she still couldn't think of anything, she glanced around the room and decided to be blunt instead. "Caleb wants to speak to you."

Fawn crossed her arms. "Since when are you in contact with him enough to become his messenger?"

"Since he came to me for help while you were in Hell. He does love you, Fawn."

"He's told me so before." Her friend shrugged. "I just don't believe him anymore." Ivy opened her mouth to argue, but Fawn kept going. "If you had your heart broken by the one person who isn't supposed to be like that, you'd understand."

Ivy walked up to her friend. "I'm not saying you have to have another relationship with him if you don't want to, but I know he wasn't lying. I can see the bond between you being stretched thin, but it's really strong on his end. It's your side tapering out. It's common knowledge emotionally separated soulmates suffer. You can fix it. Why won't you?"

Fawn didn't answer immediately. "Because he hurt me." Her voice was small and so reminiscent of how she used to be in high school before she met Dylan, that it killed Ivy to see her friend so insecure again. "And you can call it stubbornness, pride, or whatever, but I call it self-preservation, and I'm not putting myself in harm's way again."

"Speaking of harm, there have been a few developments... and I think you should hear him out—if only to hear what that news is."

Fawn closed her eyes and silently counted back from ten. "All right. But this is the last time unless I decide otherwise."

Her friend nodded. "Absolutely." Ivy paused. "He's here waiting for you in the main room, by the way."

"Ivy!"

She shrugged apologetically, and Fawn stalked out of her room ahead of her. When they reached the front of their suite, Caleb was already standing.

"Ivy said you had something to tell me."

She saw the two of them behaving like strangers and wished they could go back in time to when they looked at each other like soulmates should. Even though they hadn't known the truth back then, they had instinctively seen the other was their perfect match.

Despite the frosty tone in Fawn's voice, the two clouds of pink that constantly surrounded them was still there.

"I wanted to clear the air between us. I haven't yet fully apologized to you for everything I've done and, if you'll allow me, I wish to remedy that oversight."

"Before you start—" Fawn stood up and wrapped her hands around both sides of his head. A second passed then he cried out, startling Ivy.

Fawn released him, and he stared at her in confused resentment. "What did you do to me?"

"I broke down your mental barriers. I want you to show me your aura when you're talking."

"And you couldn't have asked?"

"I couldn't trust that. You already somehow evaded me during two Readings. How would I know you wouldn't do it again?"

A beat passed, and Ivy would have bet he was trying to stay calm. "I concede. But a warning would have been appreciated."

Fawn shrugged, clearly not caring.

"I've been a dark angel since 1854 when the Broad Street cholera outbreak killed my sister. I was twenty-two at the time. I didn't lie about that. My father had died back when I was fifteen in 1847 during the Seventh Xhosa War." He cleared his throat. "I was not so honest about my mother's death. I had tried to get medicine for both her and my sister but failed. We were too poor, so I tried to steal from the nearest apothecary. I was caught by none other than Lucifer and he said I could take enough medicine for only one dose. When I asked for a way to save both my relatives, he said he would immortalize whoever I did not give the medicine in return for my service."

"And?" When Caleb didn't immediately continue, Fawn snapped, "Are you going to continue, or are you done?" She started to rise from her seat.

"I was desperate to get the medicine for my sister, so I agreed. By the time I gave her the medicine, she was too sick for it to save her. And because there was only enough for one dose, I had not only failed to save my sister, but also doomed my mother to die."

Oh, God. How awful. Ivy couldn't imagine losing her mom. She was almost all she had left. True, she had cousins, but she had never been as close to them as her grandmother. Great, now she was thinking of that awful night and felt like she was about to cry. She swallowed past the lump forming in her throat and inhaled sharply, hoping no one heard her.

"I didn't know what to do and was completely distraught. In the middle of my mourning over my sister, Lucifer came and instead of granting my mom immortal life as I thought he would, he turned her into a marble statue. He had taken a loophole, and I was stuck doing whatever he ordered me to."

"And your job was to seduce women," Fawn clarified. She did little to disguise the utter disgust in her voice.

"Yes. And you were to be my last—you were my last. But Lucifer had offered me my freedom if I converted you to his cause. Thankfully, God took me under his care after you rightfully removed me from your life. I can't make you take me back, but I do hope you will someday forgive me. You can't know how much I regret hurting you."

Fawn stood, and he grabbed her hand. She didn't turn to face him, and her posture stiffened as if a pole had been sewn into her spine.

Ivy watched them, afraid to break up the moment.

"I want you to know I consider us being soulmates the most important part of my life. I had to get that off my chest first, because I needed you to hear me out, but the most urgent piece of news I have is a clan of Hunters has been tasked to kill you."

Shit! Ivy gasped, covering her mouth when she realized the sound had escaped. Caleb and Fawn both turned to her. She was surprised to see that her friend didn't seem to be shocked.

"I think one of them is following me. I've run into him on campus and during our movie date."

"Are you sure it was a Hunter? Supernaturals normally can't sense them until it's too late."

Fawn shrugged. "I don't know how to explain it, really. It was like I could feel the hate emanating off him and attacking me."

This was not good. "If one is after you, your life just got a whole lot more complicated. And if it's an experienced one, you might even have to go underground. For your sake, I hope it's a stupid newbie."

Caleb reached out and pulled her into a hug. "Please just let me hold you."

Ivy could see Fawn's body was still tense, and took a step forward, ready to intervene, but Fawn let her hands drop and Ivy realized her friend was okay.

Caleb spoke, "If you thought you were in danger, why are you still here? You should be halfway across the country."

Fawn pushed out of his embrace and took a step back. "I'm not dropping everything to leave."

"Even if it means you get to live?" he prodded.

"My home is with my friends and family. I'm not going anywhere without them."

He shook his head. "It's too conspicuous for you all to leave at once."

"Then I guess I'm not leaving at all."

He threw his hands up in the air. "I'm asking you to save yourself."

"And I'm refusing that request."

He took a step back and ran his fingers through his hair. "If you won't leave, may I suggest I instead remain by your side and teach you to fight?"

Fawn started pacing and didn't answer.

He retraced his steps and sat back down on the couch.

Ivy stayed in the doorway, leaning against the jamb, her eyes anxiously following her friend's movements.

Fawn stopped pacing and fixed Caleb with a stare that meant business. "All right. But just as my teacher. You deceived me on everything else, but I did learn legitimate magic during our time together."

"Are you sure?" Ivy asked. She was all for giving Caleb a second chance, but she didn't want her best friend making a decision she wasn't comfortable with.

Fawn walked closer to Caleb, who had been scrutinizing her actions. "I inexplicably still trust you with my life, but nothing more.

And if you betray me again, I swear—supernatural soulmate bond be damned—I will destroy you."

He nodded. "I understand. But will you give me permission to still hope you will change your mind?"

"I can't control your thoughts, but you know what they say about hope: It breeds eternal misery."

She did know. It hurt.

CHAPTER 15

"You did what?" Alec shouted into his phone. He closed his eyes and focused on not wanting to maim his sister's best friend. "Ivy, why would you meddle in her life like this? I thought we agreed to leave it alone?"

He had hoped that would lead to her never speaking to the lying angel again, and it seemed he might have been right if it weren't for his sister's best friend's interference.

"Well, she was miserable, and Caleb wanted to talk to her."

"Who are you to encourage her to talk to someone she clearly doesn't like? She would have gotten over it, Ivy. My sister is strong enough to withstand the heartbreak and move on. And now thanks to you, she's right back in the middle of it."

"Of course, I know that, but you have to remember this isn't a normal post-breakup funk. You know that, right? Not all girls fall into a depression just because a guy broke her heart."

"And if this goes south again? How do you think that will hurt Fawn? And affect both of us. You pushed her toward him before, but you didn't know his true nature back then. You don't have that excuse anymore. You should know better."

"It won't go wrong this time."

"How are you so sure?"

"They're soulmates."

"That didn't stop him from betraying her last time."

"You're such a pessimist. I know you'll change your opinion one day when you find your own soulmate."

Alec shook his head even though she couldn't see. Falling in love with someone else didn't completely change you as a person. It didn't make someone do a complete one-eighty. "I don't know why you believe him. What if he's lying again?"

"He's not. God told him they were soulmates."

Alec scoffed.

"What?"

"I just don't really put much stock in what he says anymore."

"Caleb or God?"

"Both. I don't take kindly to anyone who messes with my family. You know that."

"You're mad at God?"

"He certainly didn't do my sister any favors. Are you telling me you're not angry?"

"Of course, I am! But not really at any specific person, or I guess 'entity' is the right word for God..."

He couldn't help but smile at her rambling, despite his aggravation. Knowing her, she had all but set them up on the date. That made him frown again.

"Stop scowling," she said.

He could picture her standing with a hand perched on her hip in that haughty way she normally did during their arguments. "How did you know?" he muttered.

"Because you always do when you know I'm right."

He lowered his voice. "Ivy, if this goes south again..."

"I'm responsible. Got it, Captain Jackass. Talk to you later."

The next thing he heard was the call cutting off. No one else had ever gotten under his skin like Ivy did. Not even his sister.

He tossed his phone onto the bed and closed his eyes with his palms facing toward the ceiling. He imagined fire appearing in his hands and mentally recited the spell he'd been practicing. *Qui per passionem suam sit ignis.* He kept repeating it until he felt his hands warm. Only then did he open his eyes and see that he succeeded.

Despite his sister's initial accident with magic fire when they were sixteen, his mother still believed that elemental magic was the place to start. And that Fawn's and his passionate nature naturally lent itself to fire. He'd be lying to say she was wrong. But she still wasn't teaching him what he wanted most, even though he asked her every day on the phone during his lessons. How to weaponize his magic for the upcoming war.

IVY GRIPPED HER PHONE, HER KNUCKLES TURNING WHITE. "I know he's your brother, but he can be so frustrating at times."

Fawn smiled and nodded. "I've grown used to it, but yeah, I know. What did he do to piss you off now?"

"And to think he's trying to lecture me, his soulmate!"

Her friend stared at her in shock before recovering. "Wait, what? You're each other's—That's amazing! Does he know yet? How long have you known?"

She shrugged. "I've known since the beginning of high school." As shitty as it was, Ivy didn't want to say exactly how long she'd known. It would only make her appear more cowardly. And she didn't need that. "Right after I fully adjusted to being a siren, I started feeling this weird pull toward him. And I thought he started feeling something for me, too, but he never did anything. I never ended up telling him because I couldn't find a right time to do it. Besides, he thinks I'm a slut for sleeping with so many guys."

Fawn crossed her arms. "Did he tell you that?"

Ivy shook her head. "Well, no. Not specifically, but I can see it in his eyes whenever I mention a date or fling."

Fawn shook her head, a smile playing on her lips. "Thank goodness. I was about to lecture him about being a misogynistic, hypocritical jerk. He's as many flings as you do."

Ivy couldn't help but flinch. She knew it was true, but hearing it sounded extra harsh.

"Sometimes you're just as unobservant as my brother..."

Ivy's gaze sharpened. "What are you talking about?"

"He doesn't know you're each other's soulmates, but he does really like you. Oh, come on, Ivy. You've both been attracted to each other for years. I'm surprised the sexual tension hasn't set a room on fire already. I bet it could spark flames if it did." She smiled "I never knew you were both so scared to enter a relationship. Neither of you have any reason to be afraid."

"Why hasn't he said anything?"

"He was intimidated by your list of past boyfriends."

"Flings," Ivy corrected.

"You know that doesn't matter to a jealous person. And you know how hotheaded he can get."

They both laughed at that.

"Does he know you're telling me this? Did he put you up to this?" Ivy's voice was strained. It would kill her if that were the case.

"I'm not doing his dirty work. I'm helping two of my favorite people in the world get over their mutual fear." She paused before adding, "I think you should tell him soon. And that you're a siren. I'm sure he'd understand your extensive relationship past once he knows you're just trying to survive."

"I hope so. Maybe I should just give him more time. If I need you to play magical matchmaker, I'll let you know. But don't think you can escape your troubles by helping me."

"Believe me, I know."

"I don't want to be wrong on the timing..." But if she told him sooner, maybe it would make him see her side of things when it came to Fawn and Caleb. And if they were together, she could keep her cravings in check. Ivy nodded and said, "Okay, I'll tell him. Wish me luck." She grabbed her jacket and phone. "I'm going to call him back now."

"My fingers are crossed for both of you," Fawn called after her.

"Thanks," she called back. She practically ran down the stairs to the basement. It was empty. She went in and called Alec. It rang once before she hit end. She couldn't do it. Not yet. Maybe when things had died down more and he wasn't so anti-soulmate. That would be better. If only she could believe that.

IVY WAS KILLING HIM. ALEC WANTED TO SCREAM, but instead made a fireball, letting it grow to the size of his hand, and then extinguished it. It only made him wish he could hurl it at Caleb.

He grabbed his phone and called the number the jerk had given him after their last conversation about Fawn before his sister had come back from Hell. "What are you doing with my sister?" he demanded once Caleb picked up.

"Teaching her how to protect herself against Hunters."

Alec stood up, his left fist clenching. "I know I said I'd give you a chance, and I will, but I hope you know you will never deserve Fawn."

"Don't you think I know that? I would be concerned if she forgave me immediately, but is it too much to ask she keep an open mind?"

"After all the shit you put her through? Yes, I would say you're reaching a bit too far with that request." He made a frustrated sound. Why was everyone so lenient with this guy? Ivy and his mom were still trying to convince him Caleb deserved a second chance, which was absolutely ridiculous. "I didn't say this earlier in respect to Ivy and my mom, but I don't trust you. At all. But I promised myself I wouldn't interfere like Ivy unless I need to. Don't push my sister or you won't like what follows."

"I will not abandon her again."

Alec could hear the steel in his voice. The challenge was there, but for some reason he no longer wanted to punch him. If he was telling the truth, and that was a big "if," Caleb might actually care for Fawn. "Maybe you're changing after all..." But he'd still be keeping a close eye on the angel.

CHAPTER 16

IVY WAS WAITING FOR FAWN TO GET HER food when Caleb slid into the booth across from her.

"Fawn isn't here yet."

"I know." His tone was tense.

He was obviously overhearing something. "What's happening?" Right as she asked the question, she saw Fawn answer her cellphone while standing in line to pay. A few minutes passed and when she was done paying, pointed to the door. Ivy nodded.

Caleb started to turn around and she realized her mistake. "I thought you were going to approach this the smart way," she admonished, grabbing his attention again. "You're like a recovering alcoholic, always following the temptation instead of avoiding it. That is not the way to get perspective."

"But you know it's not just my fault. I've been feeling this connection almost as soon as I met her, though I didn't know it at the time. And now that she's no longer in Hell, it's drawing us together with ten times as much force."

"You think I don't know about soulmate bonds, Caleb? You forget that, unlike Fawn, I grew up with everything Supernatural. My mom has been praising soulmates for as long as I can remember, but she had it easy. If I had known they could be so much trouble—" There was *no* way she was discussing that with him.

Caleb raised a questioning eyebrow.

"Look," she sighed, "I can't tell you what to do. Right now, you're the guy Fawn can't trust to not break her heart. You need to show her that you'll actually fight for her this time."

"I'm *trying*, Ivy! I really am, but she won't let me close enough to prove how serious I am about us."

"Can you really blame her?"

"Of course, she has the right to be mad, but if she's so intent on shutting me out, how can she ever move forward? Avoiding a problem doesn't get rid of it. Sooner or later, she's going to have to face the music. Probably sooner if Lucifer is still going on with his moronic plan to attack Heaven."

"I really don't know how else to help you, Caleb."

He stood up. "In that case, I'll just go."

She had to stall him. "Hey, Caleb, can you explain something to me? I've been wondering about it since you told us your history."

"Sure," he said after a beat.

"How does being an angel keep you young? Is it like being a vampire where you stop physically aging? Or, do you just always appear young through magic or what?"

"I'm not totally sure, but I do know magic is involved. As far as I know, I stopped aging the moment I started working for Lucifer. And I haven't started again since I left his service. At least, I believe that's the case. If it weren't, I probably wouldn't be here right now."

"But that's because you're still an angel. He didn't take that away from you."

"I believe God let me keep my angelic powers because I'm more useful that way." The bitterness in his tone made her feel bad for him. She realized Caleb's position hadn't changed. Just a different boss.

"Now, I have a question for you."

"Shoot."

"Tell me about Fawn's relationship with Dylan."

That was *not* what she had expected. "They started dating in middle school. And they broke up when he moved to New Orleans with his dad after high school."

"Do they talk often?"

Now it made sense. He must have heard Dylan on the other side of the call. Angel hearing must be an awesome thing to have. "Not on a regular basis, but they keep in touch. They parted on good terms."

"Did they love each other?"

Ivy almost felt bad for her answer. "Yes, but she loves you, too."

"Really?" He seemed genuinely surprised.

"Well, as far as I can tell. But obviously things are still complicated. And neither of you are making it any easier on the other person."

"We already talked about that part." He fixed her with a knowing look. "I know what you're trying to do, Ivy. But I'm going to go talk to Fawn. She can't avoid me forever."

"She won't, Caleb."

He didn't answer, but his whole body went tense. Not a good sign. "Caleb—"

But he was already walking away.

"Don't mess this up," she muttered. She typed quickly on her phone: *Incoming. Careful, he's pissed.*

ALEC HIT THE BUZZER AND WAITED. HE HADN'T told Fawn that he was coming to visit, but he knew she should be at her dorm right now.

"Who is it?" she asked from the other side.

"Hey, sis, let me in."

She opened her door. He smiled at her and she threw her arms around him, hugging tightly before pulling back and asking, "What are you doing here?"

"You stopped answering my calls and I wanted to check on you. You're lucky Mom makes us wear these necklaces or I would have been worried something really bad had happened." Thankfully, they seemed to start working again once Fawn came back from Hell. He still wasn't sure if it was her closing her mind or Lucifer's meddling that had prevented them from working, but that wasn't a main priority anymore. Keeping Fawn safe was. He looked around and asked, "Where's your precious angel, anyway? Isn't he supposed to be glued to your side at all times? What if I wasn't me, but a demon impersonating me?"

"No one can pretend to be you without me noticing."

"Really?" Did she know how to detect them?

"They wouldn't be able to capture your signature, strange combination of lovable yet frustrating personality."

He rolled his eyes. "Thanks for that. Do me a favor and actually answer my question about Caleb."

"He's coming in a few minutes. He keeps asking to stay here over night, but I said no. Luckily, Ivy hasn't fought me on it."

"As much as I dislike the guy, I agree with him. If you're safer with him around, he should be here."

Fawn blinked. "The world must really be ending. I never thought I'd hear the day when you agreed with Caleb."

"Ha," he replied flatly. "What matters is you're safe. Under any other circumstances, I'd say you're an idiot for keeping him around."

"Thanks, Alec." Her words were sharp. "This is exactly why I stopped answering when you called. I don't need your lectures."

"I'm just trying to look out for you." Why was everyone treating him as if he was purposely trying to sabotage some greater plan? All he wanted was for his sister to be safe and happy. He just didn't happen to agree with everyone else on how to accomplish that goal.

"I know you mean well, but it's patronizing. You act as if you think I'm falling back into his arms just because he said, 'I'm sorry.' You don't give me enough credit here. Ivy thinks us being soulmates will fix everything, but I'm not so sure. Like you, I'm being careful around him."

He crossed his arms. "But how is having him near you so much not affecting your mind? If the soulmate bond really is as powerful as Ivy constantly claims it is, how can I trust you're fully thinking this through?"

"You should trust I know what I'm doing because I'm your sister. And honestly? I have reason to doubt the extent of the power of this bond because you don't seem to be affected by it at all. You're still the lovable, but slightly overbearing brother I grew up with."

Wait, *what* had she just said? "What are you talking about?"

Fawn stared at him. "Ivy didn't tell you."

"Tell me what?" he demanded.

"That you're soulmates." She sighed. "Look, what I'm trying to say is until your relationship is absolutely perfect, you have no right to tell me how to deal with my own."

He stared at her. Even when they'd fought before, she was never this mean. Had Hell changed her? Or had Caleb? Or was it the soul-mate bond itself? Whatever it was, he didn't like it.

She took a step forward. "Alec—"

He held up his hand. "Don't." He paused, took a deep breath, and asked, "Where is she?"

"At class. She'll be back within the hour. Alec, please forgive me. I didn't mean to be so harsh."

He nodded and began walking aimlessly around the room. "I'm sorry, sis," he whispered. "I just don't want to see you hurt again."

She pulled him into a hug. "I know. Thank you."

A small noise sounded behind them. Then Caleb's voice said, "So, I'm still untrustworthy, am I?"

She released Alec and rushed to the door. "Caleb, wait—"

But the angel already gone.

His sister turned to him, likely about to make an excuse, but he beat her to it and said, "You should go after him."

After she left, Alec texted Ivy: *We need to talk.*

He waited for her outside her class. She and Fawn had shared their class schedules with him at the start of the semester, so he knew when they'd be busy, and he'd done the same. They'd shared them with their moms, too, but they always seemed to call when they were in class, defeating the purpose of them having their schedules in the first place.

"Ivy!" he shouted when the students let out.

She turned and froze when she saw him. That wasn't a good sign.

He waved her over.

"What are you doing here?" she asked.

He led them into an empty classroom and closed the door. "I came to visit Fawn. But she told me something really interesting. Would you care to tell me why you never told me we were soulmates?"

SHE WAS GOING TO KILL FAWN. STARING AT Alec, she took a deep breath. "She told you?"

"Who else could have? You obviously didn't."

"I see."

"Before you get mad at her though, it came out during an argument. She didn't *mean* to tell your secret. My question is, why were you making her keep it a secret at all?"

"Because I wasn't ready to tell you."

"How long have you known?"

She considered telling him the same thing she had Fawn but lying to her own soulmate was exactly what got Caleb in trouble. "Since the first day of sixth grade."

"So, you've known we were soulmates for almost ten years and never bothered to tell me?"

When he put it like that, it sounded stupid.

"No answer? What was the matter? Didn't want to give up all the dates you were getting?"

Oh, no he didn't. "If you think that's what it was, you don't know anything about me. And it's not like you were celibate then, either."

"I wouldn't have slept with any of those girls had I known you and I were soulmates."

"Oh, really? You expect me to believe that you'd be faithful to me just because I told you we were soulmates? Come on, Alec. You've spent the past month scoffing and ridiculing soulmates every chance you got. Excuse me if I don't believe you'd suddenly become a devout believer when it applied to you. And besides, you were a teenage boy. There's no way you would have wanted to settle down with me."

"That's not fair, Ivy. I might have. I had a big crush on you back then. Maybe I would have loved for you to be my girlfriend. But you never told me. As to your other argument, if you *had* told me back then, maybe I would have been more open to it then. After all, it's not like I would have known that Fawn was going to get screwed over by hers in the future."

"But I didn't, so where does that leave us? Because that did happen. And we can't change the past."

"You're right. I can't just change my mind about soulmates, knowing how badly it's affecting my sister. And you're forgetting one thing."

"What?"

"I dated and slept with other girls because I didn't know about our being soulmates. What's your excuse?"

"I *had* to."

He let out a humorless laugh. "That's an excuse that's getting really old. Caleb says the same thing, you know."

She gritted her teeth. "It's different. I'm a siren. I need to feed on sexual energy to survive, asshole."

"Because that makes it so much better." He paused. "Does that mean you've been feeding off me and Fawn this whole time? Is that why you were so excited when Fawn met Caleb?"

"Ew, no! I have *never* fed off either of you." She couldn't help the hurt she felt at his reaction. Did he really think so lowly of her that he thought she'd been *using* her friendship with them as a personal food source? She wasn't a monster, but he was already treating her like one. She knew he'd be mad, but did he have to be so hurtful? So much for Fawn assuming he'd take it well.

"Why not? We're always hanging out, it'd be so easy for you. It's like a meal to go, for you, right?"

"Because it can have some adverse effects."

He crossed his arms. "Like what?" He might have tattooed the word, "skeptic" on his forehead.

"Too much exposure to my powers can make people act irrationality." She gave him a look that she hoped he understood.

"What—Oh. So, Jackson?"

She nodded.

"That's why you were upset."

"Yes."

He looked down at his feet. "Oh."

She repressed the urge to rub it in. He'd deserve it, too. "I'm sorry, Alec. I should have told you sooner."

He was silent for a moment. "I don't think I'm ready to forgive you yet, Ivy. I get your reasons now. I probably proved them right during this conversation, but I'm still hurt that you didn't trust me enough to tell me anyway."

THE LOOK ON IVY'S FACE MADE HIM WANT to take the words back and say he accepted her apology. That he had forgiven her. But he couldn't lie.

"Fawn went to talk to Caleb a while ago," he said. "We should probably go back to your dorm to make sure they haven't killed each other. And we should talk about what we can do to protect Fawn."

Ivy was watching him with a blank expression. "Okay. Let's go."

Once they were back at the dorm, Alec sat down on the couch. "Since no one has bothered to actually keep me in the loop, start from the beginning. Can someone please explain to me exactly what we're up against?"

Caleb answered, "They're Supernatural beings who were created by God as bounty-hunters to track down and re-imprison any of the allies and creations of Lucifer who may have escaped to Earth."

"But witches aren't created by the Devil, right?" he clarified. "Why are the coming after Fawn?"

This time, Ivy answered. "They may have been created to do good things, mainly protect humans, but they're a lot like people who use patriotism or 'the greater good' as an excuse to eliminate anyone they don't like. And I wouldn't be surprised if Lucifer corrupted them even before hiring them to kill Fawn."

"Great. So, we have some hotheads to thank for an ancient feud that created a group of people who are inclined to hate witches and therefore were happy to make a deal with Lucifer to kill me. Am I missing anything?" his sister asked.

Ivy and Caleb's grim expressions were answer enough.

"Didn't think so," she muttered and walked away.

Caleb reached her before she could leave the room. "Hey, don't let this discourage you."

She turned to him. "How can I not? Caleb, no matter how much I 'own my power,' I'm not a fighter." She put a hand on his chest. "And before you bring up the Black-Eyed Beings, that was a fluke. I have no guarantee this will end the same way."

"You're not alone, Fawn. You have your best friend, brother, and me here to protect you."

Ivy stood up. "If you don't mind, I'm going to call my mom and let her know we may be under threat again."

Once inside her bedroom, she dialed her mom.

"Hi, Ivy. How are you and Fawn doing?"

"Not so great. I'm calling because a Clan of Hunters are after her."

Her mother didn't say anything for a moment. "I'll make preparations for us and the others. Stay close to the Belgraves."

"I will, Mom. Stay safe."

CHAPTER 17

AFTER AN UNEVENTFUL WEEK, IVY FELT HER ANXIETY start to fade away. She still never strayed far from Fawn or Caleb, but she was no longer glued to their side like she had been the first few days.

Ivy was talking to her mom on the phone when she felt someone behind her. "Hold on, Mom. I'll get back to you."

Just as she was about to turn around, a hand clamped over her mouth. She tried to bite it, but it was too large. Then she was being yanked backwards and she felt something sharp pinch her neck. Instantly, she felt her body go limp and her vision went dark.

When she woke again, she felt cold metal under her arms. The Hunters had grabbed her. The thought made her jerk, but she couldn't move. They'd obviously restrained her. She blinked, but still saw blackness. A blindfold. She heard someone move near her and tensed. "You know, normally, when someone ties me up and blindfolds me, they ask me first."

"Shut up, you siren bitch. If it were up to me, I'd be killing you now. Better yet, you'd already be dead."

So, he wasn't in charge? "Then why am I here?"

He leaned in close and she wished she could lean back. "Pretty, but no brain in there, is there?"

She didn't answer.

"You're the bait."

She felt her phone buzz before it started ringing. Her captor reached into her pocket and pulled it out. "Hello, witch." Ivy couldn't hear what her friend was saying, but he said, "She's a little tied up at the moment. Will be for some time, too, but we're willing to negotiate with you. Usually we'd wipe this piece of scum off the Earth, but we're willing to make an exception just this once."

Fawn must have insulted him because the man sneered, "Do you want your friend or not?" A moment passed before he gave the ultimatum. "Give us the young witch in return for the siren."

No! Fawn couldn't come here. She'd never leave.

Clearly, Alec or Caleb had some problems with the deal because her captor began tapping his foot impatiently. She hoped they would be able to dissuade Fawn, but they clearly failed when the Hunter said, "The closest entrance to the Boston Commons at midnight. If there's any fight on your end, I can easily give orders to have your friend killed. Do not test us, little girl." A beat passed. "Good."

He slid the phone back in her pocket, his hand lingering before he pulled away. "For your sake, I hope she turns up. Otherwise, my brothers may have a little fun with you first before we put you out of your misery."

"But *you* won't?" Why was she baiting him?

"Your kind disgusts me," he spat. "I'd never stoop so low as to consort with you. My cousin was an idiot for engaging you. Just be glad I'm not calling the shots. I'd love to put a bullet through your little head."

A LEC RAN HANDS THROUGH HIS HAIR. WHY HADN'T he forgiven Ivy when he'd had the chance? Now she was being held hostage by a group of men who hated all things Supernatural, and he may never see her again. He was *such* an idiot. Why hadn't he just forgiven her? He wasn't mad anymore. Truth be told, he hadn't been after he'd had an hour to calm down and admit to himself that Ivy had been rightfully worried about telling him.

And now he was alone in rescuing her. Why had he let Fawn leave? She was better at magic than him and had walked right into the Hunters' trap. And without Caleb, he had no connection to his sister or the angel's seemingly extensive knowledge of the Hunters' protocols.

He looked at a map of the city. Where could a group of men hide two girls without attracting attention? Warehouses, empty offices, apartments, and banks made the most sense. If only he had a way to locate Fawn. A spell, or something else.

Out of the corner of his eye, he saw something shimmer. He turned and saw the Grimoire. Had it heard him? Was that even possible? He touched the cover, silently wished for a locater spell. He opened it and found the page. It had an incantation, a diagram, and instructions.

His eyes fell on the words "familial blood sacrifice" and gulped. He went into Fawn's room and found her letter opener. It had been their grandfather's and his initials were engraved in the handle. Alec highly doubted his grandfather would have ever predicted it'd be used for a magical blood sacrifice.

He grabbed a black marker and drew on the map, copying the diagram from the Grimoire. When it was done, he looked for where he was on the map and pressed the tip of the blade against his finger. He made sure to drip his blood on his location. Then he lit a candle as instructed and began repeating the words written in his ancestor's handwriting. "*Cibè àit tu air an aimsir fhàistineach tusa.*"

He watched as his blood miraculously slid across the map until it stopped moving on a large building. He looked it up and saw that it had once been a bank. So, he'd been right. He grabbed his coat and headed out. On his way, he practiced making fire. It was the best offensive magic he could do, but he hoped it would be enough.

When he got to the location, it was completely dark. How was he supposed to get inside? He saw an open window in the back and hoped no one was inside to see him go in. He focused on being invisible and silent, then looked down and noticed that his hand and arm had actually disappeared. Whoever said spells were needed clearly underestimated Fawn's power, and his own related magic.

He blasted a fireball and ducked into a large, dark basement. A bunch of Hunters came rushing in, but he aimed magic shots at each of them. They fell like bowling pins and Alec thanked his ancestors for looking out for him. He refused to thank God at this point, but he had to admit that he'd always sensed his grandma watching out for him and Fawn, even before they knew about their powers.

He inched ever closer, hoping for the same luck going forward.

Three more Hunters rushed him, and as he deflected and attacked two of them, one of them spoke into a microphone. "We have an intruder. Move the witch and secure the siren."

He'd known they weren't going to give Ivy back.

Before the Hunter could aim at him, Alec blasted him and kept moving. He moved up one floor and looked through a door to see a small army of Hunters patrolling. He felt his twin bond intensify and if he had to guess, he'd bet that his sister was being held on that floor. He had to trust Caleb could cover Fawn's protection detail until they could meet up. And for that to happen, he had to first find where they were keeping Ivy. He moved up another floor and saw only two guards standing in front of a single door.

He opened the door and they immediately turned to him, their guns trained on him. "Stop!"

He kept moving, creating a shield with one hand and firing with his other. When both of them fell, he ran up to the door and pulled it open. Ivy met him on the other side, standing and untied in *front* of the barred door behind her. "How—?"

"Caleb got me the key. Do you know where we're meeting them?"

"I'm sure we'll find them on our way out. They're one floor down."

"Let's go." Ivy grabbed his arm and started running. It was only then that he realized she wasn't wearing heels. When had he ever seen her *not* wearing heels since middle school?

"Ivy, I just want to say, I'm sorry. I should have listened to what you were saying yesterday. You were right."

"Thank you, but do you think we could do this later?" she shouted over her shoulder.

"Right. Through there," he said, pointing to the stairway.

They went down the stairs he had come up and started running toward where he'd previously seen all the guards. They rounded a corner and he saw a Hunter coming at them. He went to attack when their appearance changed, revealing his sister.

He pulled his arm back and cursed. "I almost knocked you out! You should've told me earlier."

"I was a little preoccupied fighting for my life to slip you a message."

To emphasize her point, he heard thundering of boots behind him and turned around. Fawn turned, too, grabbing one of his hands in hers. He felt fire suddenly shoot through his arm and raised his hand just in time to blast the Hunters with the newly amped up magic. Unlike the other Hunters he'd been fighting up until now, these ones had shields, and they weren't getting quashed as easily.

A few minutes later, he saw a bright beam of power knock out one of them and saw Fawn helping him until they were all lying on the ground. He went to congratulate her, but noticed her skin was paler than usual.

Caleb turned to him, "She's been poisoned. We need to get her out of here."

"I'm not strong enough," Alec said. "And our mother has a protective spell against all strangers trying to enter our home."

They all looked at Fawn.

She was breathing heavily, the poison clearly taking a large toll on her. "I can try, but I need to channel all of you."

They formed a square and linked their hands. Fawn closed her eyes. Alec felt his insides pressing in on themselves before his feet landed with a thud in the living room of their New York apartment.

Ivy watched Caleb carry Fawn toward Stella. An outside observer would think the pain on his face was from the physical effort it took to hold someone for so long, but they would have been wrong. His pain stemmed from the complete helplessness she and Alec shared with him in the situation.

"They injected her with some poison before they tried to move her," the angel explained. "I don't know what it is, but it's blocking her magic. She passed out as we were landing."

"Put her on the couch," Stella instructed. "Alec, grab water and a washcloth. Ivy, please get her some lighter clothes."

"And what about me?" Caleb asked, briefly glancing up from Fawn's weak and now limp body.

"Stay with her while I get the Grimoire." Stella left the room and Ivy gave her the clothes when she returned. Both guys looked away while she and Stella changed Fawn. Her friend still didn't open her eyes.

Stella nodded to Alec and he began dabbing his sister's forehead as it began to break out in sweat. As he did so, their mother began leafing through the pages of the precious tome. She closed it three minutes later and sighed. "I can't heal her with magic. If I were to do that, it would only accelerate the poison in her body and likely kill her."

"Is there nothing you can do to heal her?" Caleb asked. "Or at the very least slow down its progress?"

"There is nothing in here worth trying if it could harm my daughter. The poison they used is probably witchroot." They all gave her blank looks. "Have you ever heard of wolfsbane?"

Oh, no. Ivy knew where this was going.

"Of course, we have, what's the point?" Caleb asked, his tone sharp. "I'm sorry for snapping, I'm just more than a little anxious, which I'm sure you can understand."

Stella smiled gently. "This is the equivalent for witches, a very potent poison that targets the magic in our blood. The more we use our power, the worse it gets. A battle with this in one's system would have killed a less powerful witch." She put the book aside and moved closer to the angel. "She needs a blood transfusion. Neither Alec nor I can be the donors because we're also witches, and I'm pretty sure Ivy's blood may also be attacked by the virus given she is a siren and a target for Hunters. They are notoriously known for creating compound poisons for situations such as these. But there may be hope." Stella met Caleb's gaze. "Hunters don't attack angels, so they don't have a poison to harm you. Your blood may be safe."

"What do you mean may? It's not that I don't trust you, but I refuse to do anything that could hurt her."

"Putting your blood in her veins is the best shot we have at saving her, Caleb. We have to try this, and soon, or we may lose her to the poison so that even this wouldn't work."

He hesitated. "What will that do to Fawn? I don't want her to become a dark angel like me, under Lucifer's influence. I wouldn't condemn anyone to a fate like mine."

"Heal her and nothing more. She will return to her natural state as a witch. I can foresee no bad consequences."

He sighed and held out his arm.

Ivy looked away. She always hated needles. Fawn did, too, which made her being unconscious a very thin silver lining to the really dark cloud of being poisoned.

Stella waved it away and said, "I can magically transfer your blood, but it will take time."

"As long as it takes," Caleb assured.

Ivy saw Fawn begin to shiver, even as sweat was forming on her forehead. Stella lifted her hands from Fawn and sat back on her heels, visibly drained from the exertion. Caleb lifted Fawn in his arms and took off with her toward her bedroom.

Ivy stared at them and saw that the pink cloud encasing them had turned into a deep magenta. The way Caleb was looking at Fawn was as if she were his lifeline. If she'd ever thought before that he looked at her best friend with all the love in his heart since she had returned from Hell, this blew it out of the water.

She was glad that they seemed to have worked things out. When she and Alec had come back from their discussion, there wasn't any venom coming from Fawn aimed at the angel like there had been. She glanced at Alec, who was also busy watching the two of them. She was grateful he apologized, but they still had a lot more to talk about. But she had hope that, like Fawn and Caleb, they were on their way toward a better future.

"Did it work?" Alec asked.

"Yes," Stella answered. "It will take some time for her to feel back to normal, but she is no longer in any danger." She stood and walked to her office. "I'll make dinner later, after I've had some time to rest."

"Of course, Stella," Ivy said. "We can make it ourselves, if you're too tired."

She was both relieved and worried that Stella took her up on her offer. How drained must she be from all the events happening that the woman who never stopped to rest or take naps suddenly needed one?

A LEC EXAMINED CALEB'S EXPRESSION WHEN HE CAME OUT of Fawn's room for clues as to how his sister was doing. The angel's face didn't give anything away, but his shoulders were visibly stiff. It didn't look like a good sign.

"She's hungry. Do you have soup I can make for her?"

"Yeah, here." Alec led him into the kitchen and pulled down a can of chicken noodle soup. "Just follow the instructions on the can."

Caleb shot him a look. "I've been in the modern world enough times to know how to heat up soup in a microwave, Alec."

He shrugged. "Just trying to be helpful."

Five minutes later, Caleb left to bring the steaming liquid to Fawn in her room. He came back into the living room and met Alec's gaze. Alec stood up and followed him into the hallway.

Caleb spoke softly. "She doesn't know she killed the Hunters."

"We can't tell her now," Alec said. "It'll devastate her." As awful as they were and despite totally deserving it, he knew that Fawn would feel awful once she knew that she killed over twenty people during their escape.

A muscle in the angel's jaw ticked. Clearly, he didn't agree. "She should know her power."

Alec shook his head. "Wait a bit." If they were lucky, they wouldn't have to tell her at all. But if they had to, it would definitely be after she was healthy again and back to her normal self. No need to stress her out even more while she was already fighting the poison they'd pumped through her veins.

Caleb nodded once. "I'm going to check on her again." He turned and went into Fawn's room as Alec walked back into the living room. Ivy came out of the guest bedroom that Stella had offered her, dressed in a turquoise nightgown and what looked like one of his sister's fleece zip-up jackets.

She sat next to him on the couch and pulled her knees up to her chest. He quickly turned toward the TV as it flickered to life.

"What do you want to watch?" she asked.

"Whatever you want. I think I'll be going to sleep soon." The day had sapped him of all his energy, and it was already early enough in the morning that he should already be in bed. And being left alone with Ivy was an unfamiliar level of uncomfortable now that he knew they were destined for each other as soulmates. They'd always been friends, and yes, he'd had a crush on her, but this felt like he'd been told that they were having an arranged marriage. Yes, he liked her, but where was his freedom to choose his partner in life? Gone. But looking at Ivy, he wasn't so sure he was as upset about it as he originally thought he was.

CHAPTER 18

THE NEXT MORNING WAS A STRANGE ONE. FAWN slept in much later than usual, and that really said something. It was already noon before she came out of her room. Caleb, on the other hand, appeared much sooner. He sat down on one of the fabric chairs opposite her on the couch and rubbed his forehead.

"How is she?" Ivy asked quietly.

"Well, I think the poison is finally out of her system. But she's still pretty knocked out from it all."

"But she slept through the night?" Alec asked, coming in from the kitchen with a bowl of oatmeal. He sat next to her and she noticed he wore only sweatpants as pajamas. She quickly turned her attention to Caleb to see his answer.

The angel nodded.

"That's good," she said. Ivy stood up and went into the kitchen to grab a glass of water. More like fled. She closed the refrigerator and jumped a little when she saw Alec standing on the other side. "You scared me. How can you move so quietly?"

He shrugged. "How are you doing?"

"Me? I'm fine."

"You did get kidnapped and held prisoner yesterday. That tends to affect a person."

"They only sedated me. Nothing like Fawn experienced."

"But that's not what I'm asking. It's not all about my sister." He put up his hands in mock surrender. "And before you accuse me of being a bad brother for saying that, you have to admit it's true."

She opened her mouth to argue, then closed it.

He gave her a knowing look.

"Oh, shut up."

His smile got wider. "I didn't say anything." His expression turned serious. "About our last conversation—"

She put her hand up, stopping him. "You apologized. I accept. Let's just leave it at that for now." There was no way she was going to let him be with her only out of obligation to her as a soulmate. Ivy walked around Alec and had just passed the threshold of the kitchen when he answered.

"No."

She turned around. "What do you mean *no*?"

Alec met her challenging gaze head on. "Exactly that. I'm not going to 'leave it at that,' as you put it. We deserve better than that."

"I'm not doing this right now."

"Why not? Caleb's busy looking after my sister and my mom has clients all day."

"Because I said *no*, Alec."

"Why? I thought you wanted this."

"Not like this. This is the exact reason I didn't tell you before. I want you to want me for *me*."

"And how do you know I don't?"

She put her hand on her hip. "Do you?" When he didn't answer immediately, she turned to leave. "Exactly my point."

He followed her out. "Hey, that's not fair. You put me on the spot."

"You should have had an answer. And no answer still says a lot, Alec. In fact, I heard you loud and clear."

He took the glass from her hand, and she realized she'd been holding it so tightly that her knuckles had turned white.

He set it down on one of the many small tables that decorated the spacious apartment. "I feel like if I say I do feel that way about you, you wouldn't believe me right now. Truthfully, I don't know if I feel that way about you. I've had a crush on you in the past, but do I *love* you? I can't say. I've never had to think about it much before because you were always my sister's best friend."

"That's just great."

"Ivy, I don't know what you want me to say. I'm just being honest. And if you would let me finish, I was about to say that I think I could easily feel that way about you. But not immediately, and not if I have to give a final answer out of the blue like you just asked me to."

She just stared at him. What could she possibly say to that?

"I'm not asking for us to immediately jump into a relationship," he continued. "I don't think either of us are ready for it. But I also don't want to just shove the fact that we're soulmates into a box and pretend it's not the truth. Could you do that, Ivy?"

"No. You're right. We can't pretend the past didn't happen."

"That's all I'm saying."

She hesitated. What was he really asking? To let things be without forcing them one way or another. She hated the uncertainty, but it was better than ignoring their bond like she had for years. She took a deep breath. "Okay."

He shoved his hands into his pajama pockets. "So, we're good?"

She smiled at him. "We're good."

He kissed her cheek. "Thank you, Ivy." He left the kitchen and Ivy just stared at his retreating back. Well, that had gone as she expected.

"No! No! No!" Alec hit the game board, sending pieces flying everywhere. He shot a glare toward his sister. "You just had to kill us, didn't you?"

Ivy suppressed a smile. He'd always been the most competitive of them when it came to board games. Her phone buzzed, and she pulled it out. She recognized her neighbor's number and she answered. She didn't even get to answer before Maribel said, "Ivy? Oh, thank God. There's been an awful accident. Your apartment had a fire last night. I know that your mom said she was hosting family last night, but I didn't know if you were staying in the city with your friend."

She got up. Alec pointed to his bedroom and she willed her legs to carry her there. When she shut the door, she took a deep breath. "Were there any survivors?"

"Honey, I'm so sorry."

"Was 9-1-1 called?"

"I called them as soon as I heard the fire alarm, but the flames were so large and violent, that the firefighters couldn't go in immediately. By the time we were all evacuated, and they could enter your apartment, no one had survived. They said there had been a gas leak that caught on fire."

"Oh." She suspected that was the answer, but it still made her want to curl up and cry. Why hadn't she insisted on being home with her mom? It wouldn't have been a first choice to pull out of college and go somewhere else for safety, but it might have meant her mom and family would still be alive now. Instead, she'd stayed at school and all her remaining relatives were burnt to a crisp in what appeared to be a freak accident to the non-Supernatural world. But she knew better.

"Ivy, I'm so sorry. Please let me know if there's anything I can do for you."

She swallowed past the lump in her throat. "Did any of the stuff in our apartment survive?"

"I can check if there's anything, I'll put it in bags and you can come get it whenever you can."

"Thank you. I'll be staying in the city with my best friend, but you can call this number if there are any updates."

"Okay, Ivy. I'll be in touch. Take care of yourself. And let me know if you need anything."

"Bye, Maribel." She hung up and stared at the phone. Then at the door. She had to go back out there, but she was both filled with the desire to lie down and do nothing and the burning rage to watch each and every Hunter slowly drown. But she'd take kicking their asses as an acceptable consolation prize.

With that thought in mind, she went into the living room again. They all watched her, and it was their curious gazes that seemed to break the dam of her tear ducts. She dropped her cell phone and went to her knees, unable to stand as sobs wracked her muscles.

Alec put his arms around her and she couldn't bring herself to push him away and insist she was okay. Because she wasn't. At all.

"What's going on?" Fawn asked. "Is something wrong?"

She nodded and forced out the words. "The rest of my family was attacked by Hunters."

"Did any of them survive?" Caleb asked.

She shook her head.

Fawn took her hand in hers.

"I have no one left." Losing her grandmother had gutted her, but losing everyone else all at once? It was ten times worse.

"That's not true," Alec countered. "You have us."

"We won't abandon you," Fawn added.

Ivy hated the sympathy she heard in her friend's voice as much as she appreciated it. She focused on slowing her breathing. Then she disentangled herself from Alec's embrace and let go of Fawn's hand. "We need to start training a lot more."

Both twins shared a concerned look.

"Yes, but you should probably rest," Alec interjected. "You've just had a really large shock and need to recover."

Of course, he'd say that. She shook her head and grabbed Fawn's hands tightly. "You'll spar with me, right?"

"Yes. We can start now."

They cleared the furniture and took their places ten feet apart from each other.

"I'm afraid I'm too wound up to go easy on you," Ivy warned.

"Likewise. But I won't use magic."

Ivy charged and grabbed her friend's shoulders. After a few moments, Fawn was able to push her best friend away.

Ivy shot her left hand out. Fawn came up with a block and attacked her other side, but she was ready for it and blocked the hit. She could feel pure adrenaline rush through her veins and welcomed it.

A LEC WATCHED THE TWO OF THEM GOING AT it at full force and touched Caleb's shoulder to get his attention. "I'm concerned about them. I've never seen either of them act like this."

"I am too. Fawn hasn't responded like I thought she would. She seems almost numb to it."

"I'll bet she's less upset about fighting back now. I can't imagine what Ivy must be feeling right now. Or Fawn." He internally sighed.

This situation spelled disaster no matter how you cut it. "They're both so sensitive to injustice. Though I think Ivy is more jaded. I hope Fawn doesn't follow her example."

"I just don't want her to lose her kindness by stooping to their level."

"She does what she needs to survive, but I agree with you." A crash sounded, and he quickly added, "We should probably supervise them before they break something even my mom's magic can't repair."

He walked up and took Ivy's place opposite his sister and shot a stream of water at his sister. Surprisingly, she didn't block it immediately, only managing to do so right before she got drenched.

He sent more water at her, and she managed to create a magic shield, but it disappeared when the liquid reached her. "Alec!"

"What? You said you were ready to fight the Hunters. Fight back!"

She glared at him and shot a fire ball at him. He created a shield and watched her attack smash into it and fizzle out on impact.

"Is that all you got?" he taunted.

Caleb sent him a warning look over his sister's shoulder, but he knew what he was doing.

"Stop talking, Alec! Let me concentrate."

"You know, the Hunters won't stay quiet for you, so you have enough time to blast them away with magic." She shot a fireball at him without any warning. He smiled. This was getting kind of fun.

When she shouted, "I get it okay? You were right. I'm not ready to take them on. Stop attacking me!" twenty minutes later, he wondered if he'd miscalculated.

But when Caleb told her to, "Stay focused," he kept advancing.

By the end of the duel, it was clear Fawn was ready to rip someone's head off.

Caleb offered her a water bottle and towel, which she refused. "Come on, Fawn, you need to stay hydrated." They continued talking and suddenly a fireball was flying at Caleb. Alec was thankful it wasn't aimed at him.

"If I'm supposed to have any chance at fulfilling this prophecy, I need to get better, I just don't know how," Fawn spoke louder as she went on and gestured with her hands. The more worked up she got, the faster she released fireballs at him, Caleb, and Ivy, indiscriminately.

Caleb was behind her immediately, restraining her arms behind her back. "Fawn, you need to calm down."

She struggled against him. "Let go of me!"

"Not until you stop trying to burn us all alive."

They were at an impasse, the deafening silence stretching uncomfortably long. She was breathing heavily, unable to meet his gaze as he silently asked her, *Are you okay?*

Stella walked in and said, "Well, I think that's enough training for today. Why don't you all go clean up and prepare for lunch?"

The four nodded, and Caleb finally let go of Fawn. She ran to her room without another word and locked the door, leaving them all outside. He met Ivy's gaze. A beat passed before they set about cleaning up the living room.

"Ivy, can I talk to you for a minute?"

Alec watched Ivy follow his mother into her office and wished he could do something to make her feel better. But he knew that losing loved ones wasn't something any grand gesture could heal. And he couldn't imagine what it was like to lose multiple family members at once. Or in such a horrific way.

I VY CLOSED THE WOODEN DOOR BEHIND THEM GENTLY and stared at Stella. "I assume you know what happened?"

It came out like a question, even though she knew there was no doubt. Perhaps she was hoping Stella would tell her losing her family had been a nightmare. That they were still alive.

Stella didn't answer. Instead, she just pulled Ivy into a tight hug.

Before she could stop them, tears filled her eyes and were overflowing onto her cheeks and staining Stella's shirt.

She tried to pull back, but the hug didn't let up. "I'm ruining your top," she said, trying to explain.

"Who cares about a shirt?" Stella answered. It was something Fawn would have said. The similarity between the two made Ivy briefly smile before she remembered her own mom and began sobbing with renewed vigor.

Had her mother thought of her as she died? Was her death sudden or did the bastards draw it out like they so clearly wanted to do to her?

She tried to calm her heartbeat, but she felt it racing in her chest. Why hadn't she been home with them? It had been bad enough when her grandma and cousin were killed. Despite her not knowing all the details immediately after, the pain of loss hadn't been dulled. But now that she knew about the Hunters and had stayed with her best friend instead of her own *family*? It made her feel like the worst person ever.

Ivy finally noticed that Stella was rubbing small circles on her back. She slowly pulled away from her best friend's mom who gave her a sad smile. "I'm so sorry, Ivy."

Ivy felt another tear fall and wiped her eyes with the back of her hand. "I know."

"If there's anything I can do—"

"There isn't."

"Please let me know," Stella continued, undeterred. "I've always considered you and your mom as extended family, and I want to know what I can to support you. The guestroom is yours. Let me know if you need anything."

"Thank you, Stella. But right now, there's nothing I can think of. I just need to process everything on my own." She opened the door and walked back out to the living room.

A LEC SAT ON THE COUCH, WISHING HE WASN'T so useless. He couldn't help his sister because he wasn't powerful enough, and he couldn't turn back time to save Ivy's family.

He sat up straighter when he saw Ivy coming towards him. She stared straight ahead as if she didn't see him, and abruptly went into the guest room and closed the door.

Alec walked over, but saw his mom shake her head. He took a step back, but his instincts told him leaving Ivy alone wasn't the right choice. He knocked on the door.

It didn't open.

"What?" Ivy asked.

"Is there something I can do to make you feel better, Ivy?"

"No, Alec. You can't fix everything."

He knew and hated that fact. "Doesn't mean I can't try."

"I just want to be alone right now, Alec."

He took a deep breath. "Okay. But if you change your mind, I'll be in my room with the door open."

She didn't answer, but he knew she'd heard him. He finished cleaning the living room then grabbed a glass of water from the fridge and retreated to his room like everyone else had to theirs.

Two hours later, his mom appeared in his doorway. "Want to help me make lunch?"

He knew it wasn't a question and silently followed her to the kitchen. As he cut the vegetables to be cooked, he felt his mom watching him steadily.

"What?" he finally asked.

"Do you want to talk?" she asked.

He shook his head.

To his surprise, she nodded. "When you do, I'm here. You don't have to support Ivy and your sister without anyone supporting you."

When it was time, everyone came out for lunch. Fawn looked rested but was a lot more subdued than usual. Stella didn't comment on it, but he kept watching for a signal for how she was doing. She finished first, put away her plate, and then retreated into her room.

Ivy went into the guest room to grab a book and was curled up in the large fabric chair in the corner of the living room. Alec grabbed his laptop and started looking at what was coming up for him when he eventually, if ever, got back to his regular school life.

By the time it was time for dinner, Alec approached Caleb who was waiting outside his sister's room. "She should eat."

Caleb nodded. "I'll wake her."

Dinner was similarly quiet, but at some point, all of their staring must have gotten to Fawn because she said, "What?"

"How are you doing?" Caleb asked her.

"I was just tired. I'm fine." She took a few more bites, cleaning off her plate, and pushed back from the table.

"Where are you going?" he asked his sister.

"Back to sleep," she called back.

He turned to his mom. "Is that normal?"

"Let her sleep, Alec. She needs her strength and sleep is the best way for her to get it."

He didn't disagree, but it was still strange seeing Fawn sleeping so often when usually she was up and about as much as him, if not more. He turned to see Ivy walking around the apartment aimlessly.

"Want to watch a show?" he asked her. Maybe a distraction would help.

"Sure." She sat next to him and grabbed the remote from next to him, leaning across him as she did so.

He sucked in a breath and held still until she was sitting back up and turned on the TV. Now wasn't the time. "You know, just because I invited you, doesn't mean you get to pick the show," he teased.

She turned and stuck her tongue out at him. "I was going to ask your opinion, but just for that, now I'm going pick what we watch."

He leaned back, putting more distance between them so he could breathe easier. But even with the expanded separation, he could still smell the strawberry shampoo in her hair. "Fine. Pick your show."

She clicked through the channels and settled on some drama he'd never watched before. From what he could tell, it was a TV adaptation of yet another one of the overly-dramatic paranormal romance series his sister had been obsessed with during high school. He had no idea Ivy was also into that stuff, but now he wondered if Ivy was the one who had introduced Fawn to the books in the first place. He briefly wondered if she had first-hand experience of a lot of the scenes, but pushed that ugly thought away before it could take root and ruin the moment.

Twenty minutes in, Ivy rested her head on his shoulder and seemed to quickly fall asleep as her breath steadied. He was tempted to turn off the TV but didn't want to wake her. So, he waited. When ten more minutes passed, he stretched to reach the remote, turned off the TV, and lifted Ivy into his arms. He tucked her into the guest room bed and closed the door behind him. He met his mom in the hallway who gave him a knowing smile. "Is Ivy sleeping?"

He nodded. "She may wake up again since it's early, but I thought she'd be more comfortable in a bed than on the couch."

"You're good for each other."

He was glad someone else thought so. Why couldn't *she* agree?

part three

Every man needs his Siren
To check his courage and strength
When he hears her song
In his travels through the unknown.

DEJAN STOJANOVIC

CHAPTER 19

I VY SAT UP WHEN SHE HEARD A CRASH. She slowly opened her door and saw Alec also poking his head out of his room. He held a finger to his lips and they both moved forward, closing their doors. Someone else appeared in the doorway, and Alec created a magical fireball, extinguishing it once he saw it was Stella.

They moved into the living room and she saw Fawn and Caleb lying together on the bed. She smiled briefly before searching the dark room for the source of the crash that had woken her up.

Then she learned the answer when three men with guns came out of the kitchen with guns drawn. Hunters. How did they get in?

"Lucifer must have helped them," Stella said. "There's no other way they could have broken through the wards I put up."

"Well, they're here now," Alec muttered.

"No, shit, Sherlock," Ivy replied, staring at the red-clad men. She could feel the adrenaline coursing through her body, making her muscles thrum with nervous energy while her mind was excited for the chance to finally attack the group that had killed her family.

The invaders didn't move, but Ivy heard shifting on the bed and assumed Caleb and Fawn finally woke up. As if that's what they had been waiting for, the Hunters charged.

"Watch out!" Alec yelled just as one lunged for her.

Ivy moved out of the way, causing the man to hit the ground hard.

She wasted no time in kicking his gun out of reach and taking it for herself, aiming at his head and pulling the trigger. She kicked him, making sure he was dead.

Then, she spun and shot another Hunter coming at her, and aimed at one that was fighting Alec. *Get out of the way*, she willed him. She saw movement out of the corner of her eye and ducked just before a Hunter threw a punch at her head. It caught her shoulder, making her fold over. She shot him in the stomach and dodged before he could take her to the ground with him.

She took aim at the one fighting Alec as he pushed him away, and another that was approaching him from behind. Someone grabbed her hair, and she cursed herself for not watching her back. She dropped the gun, grabbed her attacker's hand and twisted under his arm, dislocating his shoulder. She heard him curse and his grip loosened. She attacked his abdomen with a punch, then kneed him when he bent over, dropping him to the ground with a thud. She grabbed the gun from the ground and shot him.

She quickly shot another one coming at her. She saw new Hunters entering and tried to move closer but couldn't get around Caleb's wingspan. Three teamed up against Stella and Alec seemed to be getting tired as he fought against two Hunters who had cornered him. When had that happened? Then she saw a Hunter come up behind Caleb and put him in a headlock.

Ivy saw the attacker's mouth moving but couldn't hear what he was saying. Then he snapped Caleb's neck. Holy—! Could angels be killed that way? She hoped not.

It seemed to break something in Fawn because her friend screamed so loud that she was surprised that the glass in the apartment didn't shatter. Then a blast of white light seemed to emanate from Fawn. Ivy closed her eyes, and hoped her friend knew what she was doing.

When she opened her eyes, she was surprised to find all the Hunters lying on the ground. Dead. She stepped over their bodies toward Alec, who pulled her into a hug. Stella came closer, too. Fawn looked up at them, tears in her eyes, as she cradled Caleb's head in her lap.

God, don't let him actually be dead.

Caleb's eyes fluttered open and Fawn began sobbing.

Ivy met Alec's gaze. *Thank God.*

ALEC WISHED HE COULD SCRUB AWAY EVERY SKIN cell on his body, trying to get rid of any reminder of the Hunters. They'd taken Ivy and Fawn, and even though he'd gotten them both back, and the bastards had permanently taken Ivy's family from her. They'd almost taken his sister's soulmate, too.

He might not be a fan of the angel, but he didn't want the guy to die. Caleb had done his best to protect Fawn and really did seem to love her. Regardless of whether his sister took Caleb back, he could now admit that he had been wrong about him. That didn't mean he was super happy about the fact that they were both staying in Fawn's bedroom tonight.

Ivy had called him overprotective and had reminded him that his little sister had already shared a bed with Caleb before. He stepped into the shower and tried to ignore the implications of that.

He rinsed his hair one more time and stepped out of the shower. He rubbed his hair with the towel until it was dry enough and pulled on pajama pants. Then he turned off the light and climbed into bed in the dark, a trick he'd learned when he was six.

Alec didn't remember falling asleep, but he couldn't have been sleeping more than a few hours when he woke up to a burning sensation on his neck for the second time in a few months. He ran out of his room to Fawn's to see what was wrong. When her door opened, and she stood on the other side, the thought hit him. If she was okay, it had to be their mom.

She grabbed his hand, and together, they ran to the Reading room. He heard the guest room door open and assumed Ivy was following them, too. He couldn't explain why, but he knew that their mom wasn't in her bedroom. And when they opened the door, he was proven right. She lay, seemingly passed out, in the center of a bloodied pentacle drawn on the wooden floor. *This was not good.* He forced himself to take a deep breath and stay calm. *Holy shit.*

Alec almost jumped when their mom sat up unexpectedly, her glazed eyes staring at them like something out of a horror movie, Lucifer's voice spoke as her lips moved. "You may have won the battle, but you will not win the war. And you," she turned to Fawn, who stood frozen in fear, "my father's champion, a murderess in cold blood. You've corrupted yourself beyond repair. How do you expect to defeat me when you're no better?"

He saw his sister stiffen and turn toward Caleb.

"Don't listen to him," the angel comforted her. "He's just trying to upset you."

She didn't answer, but he nodded, so Alec assumed they had just silently communicated.

Caleb spoke louder, addressing him, too, but he couldn't hear the words clearly enough to decipher them. Instead, Alec felt his head go fuzzy, like how Fawn often described her frequent migraines. Was he finally getting one after all these years? Then everything went black.

He woke up lying on the ground, with his head in Ivy's lap. He blinked a few times, readjusting to the dim room. "What happened?"

"God and Lucifer possessed both of you to have a nice, threatening conversation," his sister replied, still scrubbing at the bloodied markings on the floor.

He rolled over and saw that their mom was still lying on the ground. "Why isn't Mom waking up from the trance?" He grabbed the last scrubbing brush on the ground, dipped in the bucket of soapy water someone had brought into the room. It made him wonder how long he'd been out of it. But that wasn't the most important thing right now.

"I'm not sure," Caleb answered.

Fawn stood up and found the Grimoire.

"What are you looking for?" Ivy asked.

"How to perform an exorcism."

Caleb moved closer to her as if to protect her from the world.

"Are you sure?" Ivy asked.

"I have to."

Caleb grabbed Fawn's hand. "Please, think this through, Fawn. You're still learning magic. What if something goes wrong? Even non-Supernaturals know how dangerous it is to perform this ritual."

"I'm more powerful than them and the average witch. You said so yourself." She spoke more gently, "I'll be careful. But this is our mother we're talking about. I need to try to save her."

His sister began flipping through the pages. She found something and began reading. She met his gaze and gave him instructions. "Alec, can you find mom's box of crystals and the bag of aquamarine? And a mortar and pestle?"

He abandoned his cleaning efforts and started rummaging in the cabinets to find the items his sister requested. He had no idea where their mom kept all that stuff, but it had to be somewhere in here, right? The first cabinet he checked held a bunch of spices and bowls. He found a white, porcelain mortar and pestle and quickly placed them on the floor while he kept looking for the other things Fawn asked for.

The second cabinet he checked housed his mom's Reading materials. Tarot cards, the mat, and a collection of pendulums hanging from a silver tree-shaped jewelry holder. No crystals or aquamarine in sight. He closed the glass doors and kept looking.

He finally found the aquamarine in a chest on one of the lower shelves. He'd never noticed it there before and wasted no time in pulling out the matching blue velvet bag similar to the one that held his mom's tarot deck. He found a dark, wooden box with a carved mandala in the back of the top-most shelf. He grabbed it with both hands, careful not to knock over anything else or drop what he was holding. He placed it on the floor and closed the chest gently.

Fawn kept talking. "Ivy, can you get salt and a cup of water from the kitchen?"

He heard Ivy leave the room. Alec gathered the things in his arms and walked closer to his sister who was sitting in the center of the room. She motioned for him and Ivy to place their objects next to Caleb on the floor.

"Can you crush some of the aquamarine, mix it with the salt and water until it's a paste?" Fawn asked Caleb.

The angel did as she asked and held the stone bowl up to her when he was done. She dipped her fingers in it until her middle and index fingers were coated with it. Fawn then painted a runic symbol on her mother's forehead. He'd never seen it before, but he trusted she was getting it from the family-tested Grimoire.

"Ivy, can you get five candles?"

His soulmate quickly left again and came back after a minute with an armful of candles. Fawn told her to place each candle on the points of the pentacle.

Then his sister magically lit all the candles. She closed her eyes, exhaled loudly, and seemed to meditate. Or, at least try to, because a frown quickly appeared. "This isn't working." Fawn magically shut the book in frustration before putting more paste on her fingers. She put her hands on either side of her mother's head and closed her eyes again. A beat passed, and then she began chanting. "*Vade, Satana, inventor et magister omnis fallaciae, hostis humanae salutis.*" She got louder as she continued, "*Cecidit angelus, resistimus vestris malis tactus. Hanc animam purgare. Tenebris filium dei, quas eieci te ad domum inferni.*"

The words sent a chill through Alec as if all the candles had been blown out and all the warmth sucked from the room. But that was nothing compared to the fear he felt when he saw bloody tears over-flowing from her and their mom's eyes. Caleb surged forward, wrapping his arms around Fawn's waist and pulling her away from their mom.

Alec abandoned his standing position outside the pentacle, away from the spell, and ran to his mother's side. Ivy left and came back with two wet washcloths. When she came back, Caleb took one and began dabbing at Fawn's face.

Ivy brought the other over to his mom, knelt down, and started cleaning his mom's face while he held her head in his lap like Ivy had for him. *God, why couldn't they catch a break?*

CHAPTER 20

THE NEXT MORNING, IVY KNOCKED ON ALEC'S BEDROOM door. She held her breath as she heard him moving around inside at a fast pace.

"Just a second!" He opened the door and took a step back in surprise. "Ivy, are you okay?"

"Yeah. I just wanted to see how you were doing. Your mom is already up and making breakfast for the rest of us."

"Is Fawn up?"

She nodded. Ivy couldn't remember the last time she'd seen Fawn behaving so lively. "I was wondering if we could talk a little now."

That seemed to take him off guard. "Sure." He waved her in and closed the door behind her. "What do you want to talk about?"

"I was thinking about what you said yesterday and... I don't think I can be around you right now with the way things are. I think the soul-mate bond is starting to affect me like it did Fawn."

"Why didn't it affect you before?"

"I'm not sure. But maybe it's because you didn't know? We weren't actively putting a brake on our relationship knowing we were destined."

He sat down on his bed. "And now that I know, you're hurting?"

She nodded. "It's not exactly like Fawn, though. I'm not in physical pain, but emotionally, it's hard for me to see you and remember that we're not together yet. And I know that we're on a different timeline than Fawn and Caleb but seeing them happy together only makes it harder for me." She looked away, unable to meet his gaze. "Maybe it's affecting me more because I've known for so long."

"I feel it, too, Ivy. But I still think waiting until we organically feel romantic love for each other is important. That's what Fawn did, on top of making sure Caleb was trustworthy."

"And to think I originally didn't want to pursue this. You were the one who convinced me to keep an open mind. Forget I said anything."

She walked back into the kitchen and was met with the curious glances of Fawn, Caleb, and Stella. She quickly looked down. "Alec will be in soon. I'm going to have a smoothie. I don't think I'm hungry enough for pancakes anymore."

"Of course, dear. I'll make it for you. Why don't you go sit down?"

"Thank you, Stella."

A few minutes later, Alec came into the kitchen and tried to catch her eye, but she turned to Fawn. "How'd you sleep after... you know?" She still wasn't sure if Stella knew what had happened.

"Pretty well. I spent about fifteen minutes waiting for the magic to fade away, so I could sleep. But once I was sleeping, I was out for the night until I woke up. What about you?"

"Pretty much the same. Without the magic, of course."

"I hope you'll sleep better tonight now that the Hunters aren't a problem anymore."

Since they weren't what she was worried about, she doubted it would make much of a difference. "Maybe."

ALEC GAVE UP ON TRYING TO TALK TO Ivy alone. She obviously didn't want to talk about it, but how were either of them going to fall in love, especially as quickly as she needed, with the other if they were barely talking to each other?

Ivy disappeared into the guest room and didn't come out again until lunch. As they ate, Alec watched her constantly switching between talking to Fawn or Caleb.

Fawn finished first and said, "Who wants to train with me?"

Caleb reached out to her and squeezed her hand. "Love, are you sure you want to jump back into your magic lessons? You've been through a lot of stuff recently, and I'd hate for you to burn yourself out."

"I'm fine." She pulled away from him. "I really am. Everyone just needs to calm down. I'm going to make space in the living room for us to train."

"Fawn—" Caleb started to follow her, but Alec stopped the angel.

"Maybe we should listen to her," he said. "The worst that happens is she messes up the furniture."

"I've seen Fawn wired, but I've never seen her like this," Ivy said.

"That's what I'm worried about," Caleb said.

By the time they finished their meal and joined her, Fawn was bouncing on her heels with excitement.

Caleb stepped up first, and asked, "Ready?"

She nodded, and he sent a blast of magic fire toward her. Nothing happened. At the last second, a transparent, wall of magic appeared. Luckily, despite its weak strength, it was enough to withstand Caleb's attack. Before the flames fully dissipated, he was suddenly at her side.

"What just happened? Why didn't you move out of the way? I know you were trying but keeping yourself in the line of fire is dangerous, not to mention incredibly reckless."

"I don't know. I can't do magic."

Stella walked in. "It's because you're close to burning out."

Alec turned toward her. "What do you mean?"

"Witches are born with magic, but when one of our kind uses our powers so extensively and consistently as you have been recently, it becomes harder to perform magic until our body eventually shuts down that ability. It's a temporary handicap imposed as a self-defense mechanism. It safeguards a small amount of magic, so it can regenerate, but given the circumstances, being stuck in such a state now would be extremely dangerous for you."

"If it happens to her, do I automatically burn out, too?"

"No, thankfully, it is not something that can transfer through your twin bond."

"Could I give her some of my magic? Like something similar to a mystical blood transfusion?"

Stella shook her head. "Unfortunately, no. At least, not to my knowledge. I can't imagine it would be possible, or dark witches would likely try to steal others' magic."

"If Fawn has to wait until she recovers, what can she do in the meantime? How is she supposed to protect herself and prepare to fulfill the prophecy if she can't practice using her powers?"

"I don't know," Stella answered. "Unfortunately, there is no immediate remedy. I suppose it was created as a way to humble us, to prevent any of us from exercising our power for too long unchecked. I believe it would be best if she took a break from all of this."

"Now is not the time to be going on a vacation!" Fawn objected. "I need to prepare for what's coming."

"None of that will matter if you can't use your magic," Caleb solemnly interjected.

"Where can we go, anyway? We're about to fight the Devil. I doubt a change of scenery will stop him from coming after me."

"Caleb will create the same wards that are here," Stella answered. "You two should start packing now and leave before noon."

"Where are we going?" Fawn asked.

"My townhouse in London," Caleb suggested.

Wait, what? Alec had been following along, but going across the globe? Was that really necessary?

"You still have a home there?"

He nodded. "I'll go pack for both of us. You should stay here and say your goodbyes. I don't know how long we'll be away."

"I'm going to go prepare some salves for you and herbs for your protection." Stella turned and walked toward the Reading room. The wooden door closed, and Fawn turned to him and Ivy.

He pulled her into a hug. He didn't want her to leave, but if their mom thought it was the best thing to do, then he couldn't stop her from going.

"I'll be fine, Alec," she said, answering his unsaid reservations.

He wished he could believe her.

"What do you think is going to happen?" Ivy asked.

Fawn glanced toward the Reading room where their mom was busy preparing things. "I don't know. But I'll stay in touch, okay?"

"Hourly check-ins," he said.

"He's over-exaggerating," Ivy cut in, looping her arm through his, taking him by surprise. "You only need to text me every few hours."

Fawn shook her head. "You're both being ridiculous. Everything is going to be fine. We're just going on a short vacation. I'll be back in no time. Maybe even with my magic back."

Caleb reentered the living room and took Fawn's hand. "Ready?" The angel opened a portal and guided her forward. Once they stepped through, it closed behind them, leaving no trace behind.

Stella spoke behind him. "The only thing they can do is wait."

"What about us?"

"Your sister had the right idea to practice, but given the current circumstances, perhaps the two of you can instead take advantage of this pause to work on some other things." She gave them both a meaningful look before walking back into the Reading room.

Ivy surprised him by speaking first. "I was wrong to pressure you this morning. I'm sorry."

"No, you were right to tell me. I'm sorry I didn't react that well. I've never known about soulmates before everything happened with Fawn and Caleb. I'm still trying to wrap my head around it all and I thought going slowly would be the best."

"Thought?"

"I think maybe you have a point. Why deny our soulmate connection? We've known each other almost our whole lives, and I like to think that we're really good friends."

That made her smile. "We are. Even if you are a bit overbearing and crazy at times."

He crossed his arms over his chest. "That's only because you and Fawn drive me nuts."

She didn't respond, just looked at him with a happier expression than he'd seen on her in a while.

"I'm going to hang out in my room until dinner. If you want to join me, just knock."

"Okay. Maybe I will."

A S THE MOVIE CREDIT ROLLED ON HER LAPTOP screen, Ivy closed her computer and tucked it under her arm. She knocked on Alec's door, which he opened immediately. "I know we already had dinner, but I was wondering if that offer is still on the table?"

He let her in and lay back down on his bed, leaving enough space for her next to him. "Make yourself comfortable."

They hadn't been relaxing for more than a few minutes when Alec sat up suddenly. His cellphone rang. "Hello?" He started pacing around his room at the foot of his bed. "What happened?" she heard him say, his shoulders going tense. "And where were you? I thought you were supposed to protect her." Clearly Alec didn't like Caleb's answer because he snapped, "You couldn't have magically conjured them? Maybe then Fawn wouldn't be defenseless without her magic."

Fawn had *lost* her magic? "What happened?"

Alec pulled the phone away from his ear. "Caleb left her to buy things in town. And Lucifer ambushed my sister when he was gone."

"Is she okay?" Ivy asked.

Alec took a deep breath and spoke more calmly into the speaker. "Can you put her on the phone?"

The peace didn't last long. "*Bullshit.* Hand her the phone."

A beat passed, and he said, "No, you idiot. I have tact." His pacing was getting faster now.

"How are you doing? You're coming back?"

Ivy sat up at that.

"Of course," Alec said. "What are you going to do now?"

"Fawn..." He looked at his screen then threw the phone onto the bed, barely missing her. He shot her an apologetic look and sat down on the bed next to her. "Our twin bond broke, you know. I felt it snap before Caleb even called." He paused. "I keep expecting to feel her pain about all of this, and then I remember I can't anymore."

Ivy gently put her hand on his shoulder. She felt him flinch and kept her tone soft. "I know you're upset. I am too. I don't want you to think I'm not, because I really am, but what can we do about it?"

He spun to face her. "I've never heard you sound so defeated. Where's the headstrong siren who pushed my sister into way too many college parties and encouraged her to date her soulmate? You never let something discourage you."

"My best friend just lost her fighting chance to survive a war against Hell, her twin bond, and possibly her soulmate bond, too." Saying it out loud just made it sound more depressing.

"We really do need to consult my mom, though, and see if she knows of any ways Fawn can regain her magic."

"When are Caleb and Fawn coming back?"

Alec motioned for her to stand up and drew back the covers. He lay back down on his side and she climbed in on the other side. "He said late tonight, early tomorrow. She's apparently devastated, and he doesn't want her to be any more stressed than she already is. She never wanted this destiny, but I think her magic powers have become such a huge part of her, she doesn't know what to do without them." He yawned and pulled the covers over them. "It's late. We should go to sleep. The problems will still be there in the morning." He draped his arm over her waist and turned out the bedside light.

She reveled in the warm embrace and spoke into the darkness. "Goodnight. I love you."

He kissed her shoulder, making her shiver with pleasure. "Me too."

CHAPTER 21

WHEN THEY WOKE UP THE NEXT MORNING, ALEC wasn't sure how to react. They had literally just *slept* together, but it felt like they had crossed into new territory.

"Ivy?"

"Hm?" She stretched her arms, turned over, and smiled at him. "Good morning."

"Good morning. Sleep well?"

"Yes. You?"

"Yep." But only after he first spent half an hour wide awake with the knowledge that Ivy was in bed with him. He sat up quickly, hoping she wouldn't notice his reaction. "I'm just going to the bathroom."

"I'm heading back to my room. I'll see you when I'm all dressed and ready."

When they met back out in the living room on the couch, Ivy said, "You know, maybe we could just Google the solution to the problem we talked about last night."

"That might actually work."

Ivy began typing immediately and he did, too.

His mom walked in. "Look at you two, typing away. What are you both working on?"

He gulped. "Caleb called last night."

"Oh?"

"They're coming back today because Lucifer stole Fawn's magic yesterday while pretending to be Caleb."

Ivy cut in. "And we're trying to find a solution."

His mom didn't respond at first, but she finally said, "Well, that's an original idea. Unfortunately, there's nothing in the Grimoire. We've never encountered someone losing their magic before." She went into the kitchen and he heard the blender turn on. A few moments later, she came back with a smoothie. "My first client will be here soon but let me know if you find anything."

"Okay," he said, hoping he sounded more optimistic than he felt.

TWO HOURS LATER, IVY STARED AT HER SCREEN, unable to fully digest what she was reading.

She turned it toward Alec, who immediately started reading. His eyebrows raised as he got further down the page. "This looks insane. How do we even know that this is legitimate?"

Before he could give her an answer, she heard footsteps and Stella ask, "Any luck?"

"Possibly..." Ivy started.

"It's unlikely," Alec interrupted.

"Alec—"

He continued. "We found some stuff, but it could be bogus, for all we know."

Stella sat down across from them. "May I see?"

Ivy slid the laptop to her across the coffee table. Stella waved her hand and a cup of warm tea appeared. She took a slow sip and scrolled for a few moments before closing the screen.

"How do you feel about it, Alec?"

"Will it work?"

"Answer the question first," his mother prompted calmly, but with authority, her tone leaving no room for any argument.

"If it's going to help Fawn, of course I'll do it."

"Ivy, what do you think?"

Oh, God. Why did she have to answer this?

And then Alec cut in, making her wish she'd spoken when she had the chance. "Why does it matter what she says? It's my decision."

Stella fixed her son with a chastising stare. "Because she is your other half and will have strong feelings about such drastic measures."

Ivy cleared her throat. "No disrespect, Stella, but I don't want Alec to give up his magic if there's another way to help Fawn get hers back. I know it's selfish of me, but I want to know he can defend himself." The siren sighed. "I bet you hate me now."

"Why would you say that, dear?"

Wasn't it obvious? "Because I'm practically asking you to sacrifice one child for the other. No parent should ever have to decide something like that."

Stella offered her a warm smile. "While you are correct, I have always known that my children would be placed in dire circumstances that required difficult action. And I could never think ill of you, Ivy. This may work, and there might be an alternative."

"And what would that be?" Alec asked.

"Caleb could sacrifice his magic for her," Ivy suggested, both hoping Stella would go for that suggestion and that there was somehow another option she hadn't thought of.

"Why didn't you mention anything before?"

"Because filling up a half-full tank of gas with another type of fuel can cause a disastrous combustion. It would have been too risky when Fawn still had some of her own magic."

"Did you know this would happen, Mom?"

Stella shook her head. "But I feared it might, all the same."

"Evelyn didn't warn you?" Alec pressed.

His mother shook her head. "But before we jump to conclusions, we need to think about the consequences of going through with this, regardless of who becomes the donor."

"What do you mean?"

"Caleb is over two hundred years old," she began. "Without angel immortality, he'll die," Stella clarified.

"So, I'm as good as dead if I save her..." Alec clarified, "and Caleb is dead if he's the one to restore her magic?"

"I'm afraid so," Stella answered.

Ivy covered her face with her hands. Either way, Fawn would have to lose someone. And that was awful.

"Why is nothing ever simple?" Alec muttered.

Later that afternoon, once he and Ivy had broken the news to Fawn about the possibility of getting her powers back, a proposal she was stubbornly refusing, the doorbell rang.

Fawn sprinted to the foyer and opened the door. He followed her and saw Marcus, Dylan, and a girl he had never met standing on the other side.

"Come in," his sister greeted. "It's so nice to see you again, Marcus, Dylan. I'm Fawn. And you are?"

"Bailey. I'm Dylan's girlfriend."

She held out her hand. "It's nice to meet you."

After a moment, the girl returned the gesture. "Likewise."

Alec saw Caleb and Dylan watching each other with wary eyes and hoped Dylan wasn't as hotheaded as he once used to be. "This is Caleb. He's my soulmate."

The guys nodded at each other.

Dylan hugged Fawn. When he let go of her, Alec stepped in to say hello. "Hey, man. Long time no see."

"Come into the kitchen," Stella invited all of them. "I'll make everyone something to eat."

Soon after everyone had gotten a plate, Stella called Marcus away into the Reading Room.

"Can you fight?" Caleb asked Dylan.

Dylan nodded. "I learned right after we moved. Dad started my Alpha training once we had more space and fewer prying eyes."

"You're a werewolf?" Fawn asked.

He nodded slowly. "You couldn't tell?"

The news surprised Alec, but it made sense now that he thought about it. Dylan always had been good at leading, even if he did seem to get moody and sometimes edgy without much provocation.

"I wasn't exactly in the habit of using my magic back then. But why didn't you tell me?"

Dylan shrugged. "It never came up."

"What are you talking about 'away from prying eyes'? Isn't the French Quarter as crowded as it gets in Louisiana?"

"Yes, but we live near the Bayou. We also have an apartment in the Quarter for non-wolves to visit us. It's safer that way for everyone—human and werewolf alike."

"I still can't believe you kept that a secret," he said.

Dylan shrugged.

"When did you two meet?" Fawn looked between Dylan and Bailey.

"A month after we started freshman year in college."

Stella and Marcus came out of the Reading Room, both with a serious expression in place. "We have decided we need to recruit allies," Marcus began. "Everyone will stay with their significant other."

"I've been speaking with many covens, and since most have suffered from witch hunts instigated by Lucifer, many have already pledged their allegiance to us. The others are leaning toward doing the same, but only request they meet Fawn in person first."

"If they were hoping to see a magic show, they'll be disappointed."

"What use are you if you don't have any magic?" Bailey asked, eyeing her with barely concealed contempt.

Alec was ready to defend his sister when Ivy spoke.

"Watch it, dog," his soulmate snapped. "That's my best friend you're insulting."

"Girls," Stella intervened, giving them both stern looks. "Unity is key if this is going to work. Am I being clear?"

Ivy glared at the wooden table and mumbled, "Yes, Stella."

Bailey had the good sense to keep her mouth shut.

Marcus spoke up, eyeing his group. "I expect you both to give Stella, her children, and their soulmates the utmost respect. We are guests here, and grateful for it. Represent our pack well."

"Apologies, Alpha," Bailey muttered, not meeting his gaze.

"Where are we going?" Fawn asked, changing the subject.

"You and Caleb will be staying in the North East for the aforementioned reasons," Stella answered. "You should start in Salem. They are one of the most powerful covens in the country and if you persuade them, others may follow." She turned to him and Ivy. "You will be tackling California. Be careful on your travels." Addressing the young werewolves, she said, "You will go to the states near the Great Lakes."

Marcus said, "Stella and I will be going to Las Vegas, then Florida, and back home. Everyone has their assignments. Meeting dismissed."

Bailey stood up, then sat back down when she noticed no one else had moved.

"You may go get ready," Stella affirmed.

Alec stood. Ivy followed him into his bedroom.

"Isn't she a ray of sunshine," Ivy quipped.

He sent her what he hoped was a warning gaze. "Be nice, Ivy."

"I will, if she is. But I don't have to like her."

He smiled. "No one said you had to."

She looked down at the small bag she had with her. Stella had clearly moved it earlier when she was with the others. Maribel still hadn't called to tell her she could come by to get her things, and the way it were looking, she doubted she'd be able to for a while. "Well, I'm already packed. What about you?"

"Give me a minute, and then I'll be ready."

"How are we traveling?"

"I'm not sure. But I doubt it'll be via magic. Now that I know about burnout, I don't think I should do that. And now, not even my mom should be using too much magic unnecessarily." He shut his suitcase and grabbed his coat. "Ready to go?"

She picked up her bag and nodded.

W HEN THEY REACHED THEIR HOTEL ROOM, IVY WAS ready for a hot shower. She'd never been a huge fan of flying but having Alec with her made it more bearable.

As she pulled her nightgown over her head, she stared at her reflection and wondered what he would see. Tonight, would be the second time they shared a room, and they hadn't been able to talk much more about being soulmates, but she hadn't been able to feed in the longest time and it seemed to hit her full force now. How she hadn't made him go crazy yet was a mystery to her. Her mom really had been right about her soulmate being able to withstand and temper her siren nature.

She opened the bathroom door and saw Alec pacing the room in his pajama pants. "Are you okay?"

"I'm fine. It's just that—" He looked up and lost his train of thought. He cleared his throat. "You look really nice, Ivy."

She smiled as she sat down on the bed. "Alec, you can call me 'hot,' you know. It's not a bad word. I promise I'd take it as a compliment."

He sat down next to her, seemingly still in shock.

"I know now isn't the best time to do this, but since last night, I've been feeling—remember when I told you about being a siren?"

"Yes..."

She trailed her fingers up his chest, enjoying how his muscles tightened under her touch. "Well, I've been feeling restless lately. I haven't really felt it in a while, but—"

He hauled her up to his level and kissed her before she could finish the sentence. She felt heat explode beneath his touch and she moaned into his mouth, reaching her hands up to tangle in his hair.

Alec reached down and lifted her. She wrapped her legs around his waist and let out a yelp when he tipped her backwards onto the bed. He broke off their kiss, making her sigh in disappointment. But she was quickly distracted by his lips under her jaw.

She'd never felt like this with anyone else. Sure, she'd gotten pleasure out of all of her encounters, but this was on a whole new level that she never could have imagined possible. "Alec," she moaned, reaching for his waistband.

"Mm?" he murmured against her skin, the vibrations skittering through her whole body.

She tugged on the fabric. "Hurry up."

CHAPTER 22

A LEC OPENED HIS EYES IN THE DARK, THE sun unable to penetrate the hotel room's blackout curtains, except at the bottom where a small line of light illuminated the region of carpet right under the window. He turned to Ivy who was still sleeping. He leaned over and kissed her forehead before slipping out of bed and going into the bathroom.

He sucked in a sharp breath at the cold tile under his feet as he started the shower, practically jumping out of the way of the original cold spray. While he waited for it to warm up, he checked his phone for the locations of the covens his mom wanted him and Ivy to visit. At the bottom of the message, it read, "Go after sunset." That was strange. He looked back up at the beginning and realized that while Fawn and Caleb were meeting with witch covens, they were going to see *vampire* covens. Oh, boy. He didn't know much about them out-side of pop culture, but he did know that they were old and probably had out-dated social opinions to go with them. Which would not go well with Ivy, who was a spitfire despite being a siren.

Alec reached his hand into the shower and stepped into the stall. He was in the middle of washing his hair when he heard the bathroom door open again. He turned around and saw Ivy come in.

She opened the stall door and joined him inside. "You could have woken me up."

"You looked like you were dead to the world."

Ivy reached around him to grab the shampoo from the inset ledge, pressing her body against his as she did so, and poured some of the liquid into her hand. "It's not my fault I was so tired." She began working the shampoo through her hair, a twinkle in her eye.

"As I recall, you were responsible for at least half of what happened last night."

She shrugged.

He pulled her closer. "Minx." She went up on her tip toes and kissed him. He opened his mouth and tangled his tongue with hers as the shower head rinsed their hair. They kept kissing until the water suddenly turned cold, causing them to separate. They each took two towels and dried off. "So, we'll be visiting a bunch of vampire covens."

"Okay. And?"

"Well, I think you should let me do the talking."

"And why should I do that?"

"They can be kind of sexist."

"Obviously."

"And we need their help."

"What are you trying to say, Alec? You don't think I can play nice?"

"Are you honestly telling me you'll be able to listen to some misogynistic vampire lecture us without telling him off?"

Ivy opened her mouth, then shut it.

"So, it's not an insult to women everywhere, but a request to live another day."

She glared at him, but he could see the smile tugging at her lips. "Fine," she conceded. "You can be the one who speaks. But if they piss me off—"

"God save us all."

Ivy glanced at Alec, who was driving along Interstate 105. "I think that went well."

He turned and glared at her. "You offended the coven's leader before they agreed to help us. And we had to hightail out of there, so they wouldn't make a meal out of us. I definitely wouldn't call that a success. You just *had* to put him in his place."

"He had it coming. I'm surprised no one had before."

"People probably have, and are likely dead because of it. And so would we, if I hadn't blasted them all with magic on our way out."

"We're alive. Let it go already. Here's our exit."

He turned sharply, making her slide in her seat and be thankful for the seatbelt that held her in place. She shot an accusatory look at him, but he didn't pay attention to her.

W HEN THEY WERE BACK AT THE BELGRAVE APARTMENT, Alec and Caleb followed his mom into the Reading room in the middle of dinner. "What are we doing in here?" he asked, pacing. "For all we know, we could be attacked any minute and if I'm going to die, I want as much time with my sister as possible."

"Who says it's going to be you?" Caleb asked. "If it should be anyone, it should be me. I'm her soulmate. I don't know much about the ceremony, but if there's any chance of our special bond amplifying my donation, that would be our best bet."

"Are you kidding? Fawn would never forgive us for letting you die."

"Like she'd forgive me for letting one of her own family take on the job? She'd hate me as much, if not more."

His mother cut in. "Calm down boys. For tactical reasons, having an angel and a witch surviving is the best choice. Therefore, I will sacrifice myself so neither of you need to."

"No, Mom! You know more about magic than I do. Fawn needs you to teach her."

"But when I eventually die in the future, she will need you, her brother, to comfort her."

Caleb said, "No more arguing. I will be her donor. I will hope for the best, but at worst, she will still have her family intact."

T HE GUYS HAD BEEN IN THERE FOR A few minutes and Ivy had a sinking feeling in her stomach. She stood next to her best friend. "Fawn?"

"Yeah?" A beat passed. "I'm sorry."

Had she heard her correctly? "For what? If anyone should apologize, it's me."

"For what?" Fawn echoed.

"I'm being selfish with Alec. He keeps making the point Stella is the best versed in magic, Caleb knows Lucifer better than the rest of us, and you're the foretold savior in the Prophecy. He said he's the only one who could die without altering destiny. And I haven't wanted him to sacrifice himself—even if it means the rest of us can live. Which is terrible, but true."

"I don't blame you. You just started being real soulmates. I would never ask you to give that up. We'll find another way, I promise."

"We're running out of time. And they're making the decision now as we speak, so I don't think it matters to them that you're objecting."

Fawn threw her hands up. "They're being ridiculous."

"Practical," Caleb corrected from behind her.

Fawn stormed off, following her mom into the master bedroom. Caleb followed, leaving her and Alec alone. Without a word, he walked into the kitchen. A few minutes later, Fawn ran out of the bedroom, tears in her eyes. "Congratulations, Ivy. Alec will survive this."

Alec emerged from the kitchen with a glass of water. He handed it to Fawn. "I'm sorry," he said.

Dylan walked in and went to Fawn. "Are you okay? You look like someone has died."

"They haven't yet, but they will."

That seemed to confuse the werewolf. "I don't understand."

"If you're done inserting yourself into my relationship, I'd like to speak to my soulmate now," Caleb said.

Ivy was listening so intently, she jerked in surprise when Alec touched her arm. "Let's give them some privacy."

He walked into his bedroom and she followed him. "I just wish there was another way," Alec said. "Fawn probably hates me for even bringing it up to him in the first place."

"I'm the one who *found* the ritual. I almost wish I hadn't told you. I'm glad that you'll have your magic, though. I'm not sorry about that."

"I know. And I am, too, but I still feel conflicted."

Ivy rubbed his shoulders. "Everything will be okay." It had to be.

CHAPTER 23

A LEC SAT WITH IVY AND HIS MOTHER IN the living room. His mom had told him and Ivy to come back out a few minutes ago, but she hadn't specifically said why.

Fawn and Caleb arrived, and she said, "Can we do the transfer now?" The angel didn't answer immediately, prompting her to add, "Caleb? Are you ready?"

He closed his eyes. "Yes."

"Give me your hands," Stella instructed both of them, producing an athame from thin air and cut their offered palms. "Hold hands."

Alec watched from the couch as they followed his mom's instructions. "The point of this is?"

"As their blood combines, their lives and magic will temporarily be joined," Stella explained. "And then we'll transfer his magic to Fawn."

His sister cut in. "No."

"What do you mean, 'no'? Isn't that the whole point of this?" He looked at Ivy and his mom for confirmation.

"It won't be a transfer. We'll just be sharing the magic. Evelyn told me this will work," Fawn explained in a rush. "We'll both have magic at full capacity."

"Does anyone object?" Stella asked.

Of course not. If it worked.

No one said anything.

Stella continued, "When you feel your hands burning, start chanting with me." She covered their hands with her own and closed her eyes. "*Cum sanguine coniunctos in hasce formas: mente, anima, et magia.*" She repeated it three times before Fawn and Caleb joined her, their voices sounding like something out of a horror movie séance, one of those that always went wrong. He hoped this wasn't one of those cases and watched as Caleb's body went limp and he collapsed sideways on the carpet, his fall slowed by Fawn who still held his hands.

IVY STARED AT HER FRIEND, UNABLE TO BELIEVE it had worked. Not only was Caleb still alive, but Fawn seemed to glow with her newly restored powers. And was now marked with a symbol she'd never seen before.

After Caleb pointed it out, Stella examined her daughter's face. "It's runic. Ivy, please hand me the Grimoire again." Ivy picked up the tome and handed it to her. Stella flipped it open to the last page. "I've seen this before."

"It's the same rune that was supposedly on Excalibur's hilt," Caleb explained. "And Moses' staff. And Perseus' shield. Any past legend has had that rune secretly inscribed on their object of power. Some people call it the 'Savior Rune.'"

"So what does it mean that it's on me and not on one of my possessions?" Fawn asked.

They were all on the heroes' items, which meant— "You're a weapon," Ivy answered, surprised that no one else had said it first. She looked around the room. "She's not the wielder—God is."

ALEC FELT HIS MUSCLES TENSE AS A SWARM of demons entered the park from a portal. Fawn had woken them early that morning with the foreboding message that they were coming. Caleb had portalled them all to Central Park so Stella and the witches who were present and those who agreed to help remotely could create wards to protect the unsuspecting inhabitants of their city. He still couldn't believe the number of "allies" who refused to come in person. Cowards.

"We need to contain them," Stella said, reaching out to Alec and Fawn. "Our allies will be able to enter, but the demons won't be able to get out to spread their malefic influence, either."

Alec and Fawn took their mother's hands and began chanting a protective spell that came to him instinctively. A magical dome appeared over them, puls-ing with energy and providing a barrier between them and their ene-mies. But some of them managed to get inside the protective enclosure before it reached the ground, sealing them off.

Ivy moved closer to him and together, they fought a group of six demons that headed right for them. He blasted more fireballs than he could count. Some of the demons were knocked down immediately, and others took more attacks to barely even injure, much less inca-pacitate. Ivy was busy punching, kicking, flipping, and dodging the demons' attacks. More demons kept coming at them, but at some point, their numbers seemed to stop increasing. Eventually, he and Ivy were surrounded by the bodies of at least thirty demons. Alec was breathing heavily and felt like he might collapse, but seeing Ivy still standing made him stay on his feet.

He heard Caleb yell, "Fawn!" and turned just in time to see him and a demon shoot up into the air, breaking the magic dome in the process. His sister yelled the angel's name, but with them rapidly ascend-ing, they were merely dark specks in the surprisingly bright morning sky. And then he saw Caleb falling.

Fawn screamed and seemed to stumble before going rigid.

Miraculously, Caleb's fall slowed and rather than smashing into the ground, he was gently lowered. Alec turned to see Fawn staring at her soulmate intently and realized she must have done it.

The demon landed over Caleb's lifeless body and he saw Fawn take a step. *Oh, no.* "Don't be stupid. You can't avenge Caleb's death if you die the same way he did."

She seemed to vibrate where she stood and suddenly, the demon let out a piercing screech as it spontaneously burst into flames, turned to dust and then was blown away, a red smoke flying on the breeze.

Fawn ran over to Caleb's body. "Are they gone?"

Their mother nodded. "It is over."

Alec, Ivy, and Dylan approached. "Is he okay?" Alec asked.

Before she could answer, he heard what sounded like a fire crack-er and saw a puff of red smoke appear in the center of the field like something out of *The Wizard of Oz*. Lucifer stood in an immaculate black suit, his eyes blazing red. "I hate to break up the party, but I have unfinished business with your little savior."

Fawn stepped toward the Devil before Alec or anyone else could stop her. "You don't need to make a show of this." She cleared her throat, realizing she sounded like a weak beggar. In a stronger voice, she added, "We can settle this privately."

He flashed a brilliant smile and Alec wanted to punch him. "Unfortunately, the only way I can trust you to comply with my demands is if we have an audience." Lucifer advanced toward Fawn.

"Fuck," Alec muttered. Fawn was actually going through with this. "Don't do anything stupid," he warned.

"You should listen to your brother, dear," the Devil sneered, stopping mere inches away. "After all, you don't want to render Caleb's sacrifice moot, do you? It would be a shame if his death were in vain."

"I don't need to listen to my brother. I know what I'm doing. You're going to kill me anyway. I might as well try and fight back."

Another unnerving smile spread across Lucifer's face. "I would expect nothing less from my opponent. I must say, I have enjoyed our little dance, but it's grown tiresome and the time has come for you to say goodbye." His hands closed around her neck and he lifted her into the air, above his head.

Alec saw Fawn clawing at the Devil's hand on her throat before she went limp. Red filled his vision. He ran at him, only to be hit with a red light that sent him flying backwards onto the ground. He jumped to his feet but found himself unable to move, just like he hadn't been able to when he'd been a prisoner in Hell.

Suddenly, Lucifer dropped his hands from Fawn. She blasted him with her magic, and Alec wished he could have joined her. But then he seemed to *catch* the power she threw at him. "Thank you for that. I needed a little pick-me-up." Then he turned the magic back on her just as she attacked Lucifer again, sending them both flying backwards.

Fawn ran back up to the Devil and grabbed his chest with both hands. Alec suddenly felt his necklace turn ice cold against his chest. His gaze was drawn upward when he noticed that the wards were disappearing... into his sister. As if she were channeling all the magic. And then, as if he were being petrified, Lucifer's body went completely still and paled into a marble statue. Staring at her handiwork, she created a titanium baseball bat and held it out. "If anyone needs to take out their frustration."

Alec stepped forward. "Won't that set him free?"

"No. He will never be a problem again."

He didn't need to be told twice. Alec grabbed the piece of metal and began smashing the statue with all his might. When his arms felt like they might fall off, he handed it to Ivy. He watched her go to town and bet that was for sending the Hunters after her and her family. When his soulmate offered the bat to his mom, she declined. Ivy then held it out to Dylan who put his hands up.

"No thank you," his childhood friend said.

His sister took it again and finished off what was left until there was a pile of dust where Lucifer once stood.

It was finally over.

I VY FELT HER HEART BREAK AT THE SIGHT of Fawn shouting at Caleb's dead body. She pressed herself into Alec's side, needing to feel his body warmth to remind her that he had survived the long fight. His arm came up around her waist and she realized he needed the reminder too.

Suddenly, she felt as if she were being compressed and found herself back in the Belgrave apartment. She looked at Stella who pointedly looked at her daughter. Fawn must have transported them.

An old man with a walking stick wearing all white was also there. "Fawn," the stranger said.

Fawn glared at the man. "I fulfilled your stupid Prophecy, after suffering so much for your cause—one I didn't even sign up for. You owe me big time."

Ivy realized the man must be God.

He replied, "I do."

"Bring him back," Fawn demanded. She pointed at him. "And don't you dare say you can't—or won't. It's the least you could do for me after everything I've suffered."

"As you wish."

Ivy suppressed a gasp when a transparent version of Caleb, his ghost, appeared by God's side.

Rather than being happy like she expected her to be, Fawn snapped, "Is this some kind of sick joke?"

"What do you mean?" God asked.

"You've manipulated me my whole life, and Caleb's, too, by making that deal with Lucifer in the first place, and now we don't get to be with each other? You're not only going to let him be ripped away from me, but also taunt me with a ghost version I can never touch?"

God shook his head. "I admit I have not done right by you in many ways, but I am not cruel. Look at him," he said, gesturing to the ghostly Caleb as it merged with his body.

A few moments passed before Caleb opened his eyes and Fawn threw herself at him. "You're alive!"

Alec squeezed Ivy's waist and she turned her head into his neck. He wrapped his other arm around her, holding her as she listened to his steady heartbeat.

Caleb and Fawn spoke softly before Ivy heard the unmistakable sound of kissing. A moment passed, and her friend said, "Thank you."

"If that is all you require of me..." God started.

"Will we be safe?" Fawn asked.

Ivy turned in Alec's arms to see the conversation, curious.

"Yes," the Deity said. "The whole world will be."

"Does that mean there won't be Evil anymore?"

He shook his head. "No. You defeated my son, not Evil in its entirety. Don't worry, that is not your responsibility," he added quickly.

"Thank God," she sighed.

He laughed. "You're welcome."

"Do I have my magic back from Lucifer? I don't want to put Caleb in danger again by sharing his powers."

"You are back to your original state before my son meddled with your abilities," God explained. "You have fulfilled the final part of the prophecy: United, together as one, through love, darkness shall be overcome. I'm proud of you both." He pointed to Fawn's forehead and pulled white light from where her mark had been back into his hand. God bowed to her and disappeared in a cloud of white smoke.

Fawn finally released Caleb. Ivy and Alec were immediately at their side along with Stella, Dylan, his dad, and Bailey. The others who had fought with them hadn't come back to the apartment and probably were already headed home by now.

Suddenly, flutes of champagne appeared in all of their hands. Ivy looked over at Stella who raised her glass and said, "To our victory."

"It was a long time coming," Alec added.

They clinked their glasses and drank.

"Where will we go from here?" Fawn asked.

"Wherever you want," Stella said. "After you finish college."

Alec rolled his eyes. "Yes, Mom."

"I'm sure God will help in organizing that," Caleb said. "At least you only have to make up two years instead of four."

He made it sound so simple. "But it's Junior and Senior year—there's so much work involved," Ivy muttered.

Dylan walked over. Alec hugged his best friend, giving him a hard pat on the back before they separated. Then Dylan addressed Ivy. "It was nice to see you again. Keep him out of trouble."

She smiled. "Same here. And don't worry, I will."

Marcus walked over to them. "It was an honor to fight beside both of you. And Ivy, I'm sorry to hear about your family."

She nodded. "Thank you."

Bailey came up to her. "You're not so bad, Ivy."

"It was nice to meet you."

The female werewolf said goodbye to Alec before walking over to Fawn and Caleb. She, Dylan, and Marcus left.

Then it was just the five of them.

Ivy smiled when she saw Caleb carry Fawn into their shared bedroom and close the door. They deserved it.

"I'm going to say goodnight," Stella said.

"You two, feel free to sleep in tomorrow."

"That won't be a problem, Mom," Alec said.

Stella nodded and retreated to her bedroom.

Ivy turned to Alec. "Are you tired?"

"A bit." He examined her expression. "But I think I can stay awake a little while longer if you can."

She smiled up at him. "I thought you'd never ask."

CHAPTER 24

THAT WEEKEND, ALEC TURNED TO IVY AND SAID, "I want to take you on a date."

She turned to him. "Really? Where are you taking me? And don't say a movie and then dinner."

Alec gave her a look. "I'm more original than that." Now, he just had to think of where to take her before they headed their separate ways to finish the college year. With all they had to make up, their summers were going to be killer. It was too cold to go to a beach, or even dinner under the stars. But perhaps he could do something else water-related.

"I'm glad to hear that." She leaned her head against his shoulder. "Oh, come on. You know I'm only teasing you. I'm very excited. What should I wear?"

"A swimsuit. And something nice for dinner, but nothing too warm."

"Alec, it's winter break. Do you want me to freeze?"

"Wear a warm coat and you'll be fine. Besides, you'll warm up during the date."

That caught her attention. She narrowed her eyes at him. "What are you planning, Alec Belgrave?"

"A surprise that I hope you'll like. I think we should leave here at five. Then we'll have dinner at seven."

"Where are we going that it takes two hours to get there?"

"Nowhere," he answered. "It takes one hour to get there."

"What are we doing before dinner then?"

"That's the surprise," he said. "Now, stop asking questions. I'm not telling you anymore."

T HAT NIGHT, WHEN ALEC PRESENTED HER WITH A blindfold, she looked at him like he was crazy. "You can't be serious."

"I can't trust you to not peek."

She glanced at the driver sitting in front of them. Alec had called the car before she could glimpse the destination. She turned to Alec and hissed, "You expect me to stay blindfolded for a whole hour while we travel? Now I know you really must be crazy."

"But you love me anyway and will do this for me."

"You're really insistent on this, aren't you?"

"It's just for the surprise. I won't let you fall, Ivy."

She closed her eyes. God, she hoped she didn't regret this. "Okay." She turned around and he lay the fabric over her eyes. "But if you lead me into a wall, I won't forgive you."

He tied the ribbons in a bow behind her head. "That's fair."

They talked about their upcoming months. She wasn't sure how much time passed before the car finally stopped.

Alec moved, pulling her closer to the door. "Duck," he said, lightly pushing on her head as she left the car. "Step. Okay, walk straight. I'll open the door for you."

She felt a coolness meet her as she passed through the door. She shivered in the air-conditioned room. She heard her heels clicking on the floor and realized that wherever they were, it was fancy. Alec continued to guide her forward. Ivy he heard an elevator ding and walked into it with Alec. "Can we take this off now?"

"Almost."

The elevator pinged as it climbed the floors. She heard it open and close a few times as more people entered the compartment.

"First date," she heard Alec say, probably explaining the blindfold.

A woman spoke, "Ah, it's so nice to see a young couple out and giving each other grand gestures. Do you remember when that was us, Malcolm? So, in love."

A man, presumably Malcolm, replied, "We still are, dear."

The elevator dinged, and Alec said, "This is us. It was nice meeting you both."

"Yes, yes, of course. Have fun, dear. He's clearly a keeper." Ivy knew the woman had said the last part to her.

He ushered her out and she heard the elevator doors close. Then she felt his fingers tugging at the bow. The blindfold fell away, and she saw a dimly lit pool before her. The water reflected what little light there was, making the whole space look as if they were in an aquarium. On the far edge, she saw a table with a white table cloth, lit candle, and two upholstered chairs.

She turned to Alec. "I love it."

"I'm glad." He took her coat. "I thought we could swim first and then eat."

He didn't have to tell her twice. She placed a hand on his shoulder and stepped out of her heels. Then she reached for the hem of her dress and pulled the fabric over her head, revealing her bikini underneath.

Alec sucked in a breath and she looked over her shoulder at him as she folded her dress, picked up her discarded shoes, and walked over to the table barefoot. She placed them on and under the chair. She saw Alec had also changed out of the clothes he was wearing and wore only swim trunks.

"Should we be expecting company?"

He shook his head. "I rented the place."

"For one night? That's—" extreme.

"They remembered you when I gave your name. They were happy to have us back."

She rolled her eyes. "I can't imagine why. My mom paid a lot for that party."

Alec stepped into the pool and held out a hand. "Apparently, they've gotten a lot of business for pool parties by using some of the photographs in their advertising material."

Was that how the Hunters had found her and her mom? "Ah," was all she said. She looked at his hand and instead walked to the deep end. She dove into the water and swam toward Alec. When she resurfaced, he smiled at her. And then he splashed her in the face.

"Alec!"

He grinned, went under, and swam away as she chased him. She grabbed his foot, pulled him down, and climbed up his body to reach the surface. Ivy got in one big breath before he tugged her back under.

Together, they rose at the other end of the pool. Leaning up against the pool's tile edge, Alec turned to her and asked, "So, are you happy?"

"This is amazing," she admitted. When she'd challenged him to be original, she hadn't expected he'd do anything this elaborate.

"I'm glad you approve."

She looked at him. "You had to know I'd like it."

Their bodies were so close that he had to pull back to talk to her. "I thought so, but with you I'm never entirely sure."

His tone was hard to read. "Is that a good thing?"

"Yes, it is. At least, I think so. It keeps things interesting."

"At least I entertain you."

He brought one hand to her hip, pulling her close against him. "And I don't?"

She wrapped a leg around his hip and wrapped her arms around his neck. "You do."

He moved his hand to cup the back of her knee. To her disappointment, he lowered her leg. "Cameras, Ivy."

She pushed at his chest. "You're no fun." She kicked off from the wall and swam to the other side, the water sliding across her body as she cut through it. It made her relieved to be back in the pool after so long of not being able to swim.

Ivy continued to do laps, seeing Alec doing the same whenever she turned her head for air. She gave herself into the motion, losing count after her twentieth length of the pool. She kept going until she felt her muscles getting sore. Ivy swam one last length to the shallow end.

When she reached the wall, she held onto the handle and walked up the steps to where she sat, watching Alec come toward her. He climbed out. She gathered her hair to one side and wrung out the water.

"Look at you, little mermaid. I didn't think you'd ever stop."

"Siren, Alec. I'm not a fairytale creature. And you weren't so bad. I didn't know you liked to swim."

He shrugged. "I took it up at school. It's an easy way to stay in shape. Besides, it lets me clear my mind."

"It does, doesn't it?"

He walked over to a rack of towels and handed her one. He wrapped the other around his hips. "They said that there are showers through here." She followed him through a doorway.

"Will you shower with me?"

He checked the clock on the wall and shook his head. "The food should be here soon."

"You're not making it, Alec. They can set it up while we have some alone time. Swimming has my adrenaline levels pumping now."

He smiled. "You're trying to tempt me."

She brushed her body against his. "Is it working?" She felt as much as she heard his sharp intake of breath before he pulled her and kissed her. He maneuvered her into one of the shower stalls, pulling aside the curtain and closing it again.

He reached behind them and started the water. She bit his lip when the coldness covered them. Then she licked and kissed it once the water heated up.

Alec licked the seam of her mouth and she opened for him, welcoming his warm tongue. He reached down and lifted her legs, wrapping them around his middle. She grasped at the bathroom wall behind him, kissing both sides of his jaw before fusing her lips to his yet again.

WHEN THEY WERE DRESSED AND SEATED AT THE table, their dinner in front of them, Alec asked, "What is it about showers?"

Ivy smiled at him and took a bite of the cod. Her moaning at the taste had him shifting in his seat. "Maybe it's the company." She winked, and he suppressed a smile.

"Could be. I take it you like the meal?"

"It's delicious. I didn't really get to eat much of their food last time I was here."

"I didn't know."

"How could you have? You left early." She fixed him with a curious stare. "Why did you, anyway?"

Was it safe to say his name? "I met Jackson."

She put down her fork. "And he told you we had dated."

"And Fawn told me that all of your male guests were also exes."

Ivy took a slow sip of water and he waited for her response. "Oh."

"I admit, I didn't handle it that well back then." He looked down, unable to meet her gaze. "I was a little jealous."

"Of what?" She leaned forward. "Alec, they were my ex-*flings*."

"It didn't matter. And I didn't know why, so I left to get myself under control."

"Did it work?"

"You tell me."

She smiled and held up her glass. "Well, I'm glad it didn't work."

"I'm sure you are. And so am I." He clinked his glass with hers.

THE NEXT DAY, THEY WERE ALL PACKED TO go to school. Going back to college wasn't going to be fun but knowing that Lucifer was no longer coming after Fawn or anyone else she loved made it much more bearable for Ivy. Alec, on the other hand, was very vocal in his annoyance at going back to school. It seemed to have hit him the hardest when they woke up that morning because up until now, he had barely complained about it. Maybe he secretly wished Stella would have changed her mind on the matter. She brought her bags out into the living room as Alec and Fawn talked to their mom.

"See you for Summer Break," she heard him say as she walked up to them.

"Unless we do summer school," Fawn added, stepping up beside him, earning a look of mock horror from him. Ivy suppressed the urge to tease him. Truth be told, she shared his opinion and she wasn't about to make a hypocrite of herself.

"Be safe," Stella said.

"That's easy now," Ivy said. Those were words she never thought she'd say once she learned how Caleb had betrayed Fawn. That all felt like ages ago. Had it really only been a matter of weeks?

Stella smiled at all three of them. "Still, take care of yourselves."

"Alright, Mom," Fawn and Alec said in unison. They hugged her, then Caleb came out of her friend's bedroom and they left together.

"Goodbye, Stella," Ivy said. "I'll see you at the end of the semester."

"Call me if you need anything."

"Thank you. I will."

Alec pulled her in for a kiss and she only had a moment to be embarrassed that they were making out in front of his mom before she was swept away in the sensations.

"I'm going to miss you," he whispered against her lips.

"Me, too."

That evening, just as she was unpacking in her shared dorm with Fawn, she got a phone call from her best friend. "Hey, Fawn. Where are you? I thought Caleb was bringing you back here."

"He surprised me by taking me to London. That's why I'm calling you, actually."

"Let me guess, you won't be back tomorrow, either." Magical travel really *was* amazing. A trip across the pond in less than an hour? Absolutely insane.

"Yes, but—Ivy, he proposed."

She almost dropped her phone. "Oh my God! Tell me all about it!"

"Well, he did it during the intermission of *Les Misérables*—"

"Don't tell me you've already converted him to your musical theater obsession already. I thought he was stronger than that."

"Ha ha," her friend deadpanned. "And there was this nice older couple who were basically our peanut gallery. Anyway, he gave me a ring. You're going to die when you see it." She heard her best friend yawn. "Anyway, it's almost midnight here, but I wanted to tell you as soon as the show ended."

"I'll let you sleep but thank you for telling me. Congratulations! Alec is going to flip out. I'm calling him first thing tomorrow your time so don't tell him, please."

"I promise. Sleep well. See you later this week?"

"Definitely. Goodnight, Ivy."

CHAPTER 25

A YEAR AND A HALF LATER

THE GIANT CROWD MADE IT HARD TO PINPOINT his family and Ivy, but Alec smiled, knowing they were here to support him. He'd already been to Boston, a few days before, but he didn't expect to be so nervous and simultaneously a little sad about permanently leaving school.

He hadn't been sitting with his class long when his name was called by the dean of his university. He willed himself not to trip as he walked the short trip to the podium, accepted his diploma, and flipped the side of his tassel. Sitting back down, he settled in for the long list of the rest of his classmates to cycle through, hoping he didn't fall asleep in the process.

It was almost another two hours before he found himself walking back into the college's main auditorium where his family was waiting for him.

"I'm so proud of you." Stella held her arms out to him. He went up to her and hugged her.

"Congratulations, big brother," Fawn said, patting his shoulder.

Caleb, for once, wasn't standing next to her. "He's meeting us there," she said, answering his unspoken question.

Ivy beamed at him. "You did it!"

He didn't bother to answer, instead pulling her in for a kiss. It had only been weeks since he'd last seen her, but it felt like an eternity.

Still embracing him, she asked him, "How did you stay awake?"

"I have no idea."

"Let's head to the restaurant," his mom said. "Everyone should be arriving there soon."

IVY WALKED BETWEEN FAWN AND ALEC, MORE EXCITED than she could easily justify. She was just so happy to see him again.

"We can drink this time around," she said.

Fawn smiled. "Yes, Ivy. We know."

She lightly pushed her best friend. "Come on, you're not telling me that you're not excited to drink with your family for the first time?"

"Well, we had—" He cut himself off. They had missed Thanksgiving, instead opting to stay on campus to get ahead on school work. Strange how he hadn't even noticed that before now. "Yeah, I guess I am, now that I really think about it."

"What are you ordering?" Fawn asked. "I already know mine."

"Of course, you do," he replied. "You always order the same thing. Where's your sense of adventure?"

"My taste buds like to stick with what they know."

"Boring."

His sister glared at him and Ivy couldn't help but smile. Being at separate schools always made them extra eager to tease each other once they were reunited. It was like being able to see each other in person reinvigorated their sibling rivalry in a way that phone calls and video chats couldn't. To an outsider, they looked like they had a difficult relationship, but Ivy knew it was how they showed their sibling love.

She'd been taking up more of their conversation time than usual, what with her and Alec doing the long-distance relationship thing. She was so glad to be able to kiss him again, although she hadn't been able to all day.

Her thoughts must have been obvious because Alec leaned over and kissed her gently. She closed her eyes and reveled in the warm feeling that quickly spread through her body. "I've been meaning to do that," he whispered when he ended the kiss.

"Me, too."

Fawn cleared her throat. "Remind me to thank you, brother, for stealing all of my best friend's time these past two years of school. If she wasn't studying, she was chatting with you."

"I think you'll find that *you* stole my soulmate. That was a done deal way before you ever became friends."

"But *you* didn't know that."

"Relax, you two," Ivy said, "There are enough hours in the day for me to spend time with both of you. But I'm flattered I mean so much to you both."

"False modesty doesn't suit you."

She smiled. "You're right."

A LEC SMILED AT ALL HIS FAMILY MEMBERS GATHERED at the dinner table. For the third time ever, he was graduating from a school, and keeping with tradition, his mom had invited all their family members to one of their favorite restaurants to celebrate.

"Congratulations to Alec and Fawn!"

He raised his glass to meet everyone else's, clinked with his sister on his left and Ivy on his right, then he reached for his mom's glass next to Ivy's and Caleb's, who was sitting on Fawn's other side.

"I can't believe we're free," Fawn said.

"Neither can I," Ivy added.

Alec took a long sip of his drink then put down the glass. The pomegranate margarita was the restaurant's specialty, and he was glad to be drinking it along with the rest of his relatives this time around. "I swear, I thought that last round of finals was going to drive me crazy."

The girls nodded in agreement.

"So, are you excited to start working at the bookstore?" he asked his sister. They had barely talked once their study periods had started and she had received the news that she'd gotten the job midway through their 48-hours of silence.

"I'm *so* excited. I can't believe I actually get to work around books all day."

"You must be in Heaven," Ivy said.

"Not quite," Caleb said.

They all shared a secret look, knowing how true that statement was, unbeknownst to the rest of his family.

"But for a bookworm like me, it's pretty damn close," Fawn said.

"And it's paid," Stella added.

"Lucky," Alec muttered. He was fortunate enough to get an internship as a research assistant for his favorite professor, but he'd be lying if he didn't admit that he wanted a paycheck, too.

Two of their cousins came over and clapped him on the back. "Congrats, you two. You're finally just like the rest of us. Able to drink, out of college, and wishing people could pay us just for existing."

The other nodded. "And now, we can hang out a lot more."

"You're right," he replied, "I haven't seen your dog in forever."

She glared at him. "Maybe I'll tell her to bite you the next time you come to visit."

"Peanut loves me too much."

"We'll see."

"Congratulations again, you guys," their other cousin cut in. "Are you going to hibernate for a week now?"

"More like a month," Fawn said.

"You deserve it. We'll be over there," their cousins pointed back to their seats on the other side of the table. "But we're going out for drinks after if you want to join us."

After *this*? All he wanted to do was sleep. Well, that and one other important thing. "We'll—"

"Be there," Ivy cut in.

"Great! See you all later, then."

When they were gone, he turned to her. "Really?"

"Come on, Alec. None of us have been able to party in weeks." She sent him a knowing look as a smirk played on the edge of her lips, threatening to turn into a smile. "We don't have to stay very long."

He sighed. "Fine, we'll go. But only for an hour. Two, tops."

She kissed him. "I knew you'd see it my way."

IVY DANCED WITH ALEC, HIS HANDS ON HER hips as the music flowed through her. She'd always felt energized when she used to come to parties to feed, but now it was so much better than she could ever imagine.

He leaned down and spoke in her ear. "When this song ends, I need to ask you something."

She nodded and held his face in her hands, pulling him in for a kiss. He met her fervor, his tongue licking the seam of her mouth. She opened to him immediately. Kissing had always been so simple, a prelude to bigger and better things, but with Alec, she could spend forever kissing.

The song slowed and the next one began. He took her hand and led her to the group of tables they had claimed along with his cousins. He took a seat and she decided to sit on his lap rather than move her coat and purse.

She waited for him to speak.

"Ivy, I wanted to ask you something."

She smiled. "You already told me that."

"Right." He cleared his throat. "I was wondering if... you would like to move in with me."

He said the last words in such a rush, Ivy wasn't sure she had heard him correctly. "You're asking me to move in with you?"

"Yes." He drew the word out as if he wasn't sure she was open to the idea. "It's a two-bedroom apartment in Brooklyn. It's near a subway so you could come into Manhattan whenever you want." He looked up at her, looking more nervous than she'd ever seen him before. "So, will you move in with me?"

If she hadn't already been sitting on his lap, she would have tackled him with a hug. Instead, she settled for hugging her soulmate tightly.

His hand settled on her back, pressing her against him. "Can I take that as a yes?"

"Of course, it's a yes!" She kissed him, needing to taste him again. She pulled back. "Do you already have a bed there?"

He nodded. "My mom got it set up last week."

She shifted on his lap and smiled. "Want to leave early?"

"I've been waiting for you to ask me that." He lifted her off his lap and helped her into her jacket before shrugging into his own. "Let's go."

A LEC UNLOCKED THE DOOR AND LET IVY INTO the surprisingly spacious apartment. He knew he had the high ceilings and open floor plan to thank for that. He also knew that once Ivy brought her stuff in, it would feel much smaller, a cozier home for them both.

He closed the door behind them and watched her take it all in. "What do you think?"

"It's beautiful. But you can give me the tour later." She grabbed his hand and made a beeline for his room, which was not decorated all in blue like his childhood room, but in a silvery blue that looked almost gray in some lights.

She looked at the bedspread. "I like the color." She stepped close to him, her chest brushing his with every inhale. "It's sexy." She reached behind her neck and he heard the zipper a second before she dropped her dress to the floor.

He sucked in a breath as he took in her naked body. Had he known she was only wearing that dress, he would have turned down the club invite. It had been a while since they'd last been together and it was hitting him full force now that they finally had the opportunity again.

She undid his tie and quickly unbuttoned his shirt. He discarded it on the floor and took off his pants faster than he ever had before. Ivy walked backwards until she lay on the king-sized bed. He followed her. It was times like this that he could understand how others constantly felt around his siren soulmate. She was truly irresistible. And he was so lucky she was his.

"Are you just going to stare at me? Or are you going to do something about *that*?" Her eyes dropped below his waist.

Oh, she was going to pay for that. He climbed onto the bed and kissed the corner of her mouth. Then the other and he moved down to the underside of her jaw, her throat, and her chest.

During his exploration, she wrapped her legs around his waist. He groaned against her skin and lightly bit her earlobe in warning.

"Alec..."

"Ivy," he rasped, not bothering to hide the desire he felt. It required too much energy to be anything but honest right now.

"We can go slow later."

"Okay." He kissed her and gave her exactly what she wanted.

CHAPTER 26

A MONTH LATER, ALEC TURNED HIS HEAD AND SAW the sleeping form of Ivy. He smiled. Never in a million years would he have dreamed this is where he would end up. His best friend was his soulmate, and though it took forever, they were living together. They'd fallen into such a pattern of comfortable existence that one would have thought they had done it for years.

Carefully, he slipped out of bed and grabbed his phone off the night table. Checking the time, he knew it was okay to make the call he'd been considering for a few weeks. He tapped the name from his contacts list and said, "Caleb, are you there?"

"Yeah. What can I do for you? Do you need to talk to Fawn?"

"No. It's just something I have to ask you."

"Sure, what is it?"

"When you proposed to my sister..." He looked over his shoulder to make sure Ivy was still asleep. "When did you know you wanted to ask the question?"

Silence met him, and he wanted to take back the words.

"I don't know how to explain it," his sister's soulmate said slowly. "After everything we went through, I just decided to not hide any of my feelings from her."

"That makes sense. It's just, I've been with Ivy for a while, but I *just* asked her to move in with me."

"I can't speak for you, nor would I given I know how much you and Fawn hate that, but all I can say is that you'll know in your gut."

Alec blew out a breath. That wasn't *quite* the helpful advice he had been hoping for. The angel had been alive for over a hundred years and that was all he got?

Apparently, he heard his thoughts because Caleb said, "It may be cliché, but it's truly indescribable, Alec. It'll come to you in the moment and everything will fall into place for you."

"And if it already has?"

"Then you know what you need to do. But there's no rush, Alec."

"Thanks, Caleb. Tell my sister I say hi."

"You could tell her now."

"I know you're both in wedding crunch time. Last seven days and all. I don't want to bother her, but thanks for your help."

"No problem. Good luck."

He hung up the phone and went back into the bedroom. Luckily, she was still sleeping. He wrapped his arm around her waist and gently pulled her back against his front. She made a small sound and curled further into her fetal position. It was so ironic that she always fell asleep wrapped around him, and in the morning, she was the exact opposite.

He didn't remember falling back asleep, but when he woke up again, Ivy was hovering over him, a mischievous glint in her eye.

"Good morning," he said.

"About time you woke up sleepy head."

He smiled. "Sorry to have kept you waiting."

"As you should be." She kissed him, and he gave himself over to her.

I VY SAW FAWN AND SHOVED DOWN THE URGE to tear up. There was no way she was going to cry in a bridal shop for a dress that wasn't even her own. At least, that's what she told herself.

Her best friend turned around. "What do you think?"

"As if you have to ask."

Fawn beamed. "You're right. I just wanted to see your reaction."

"You would have seen it months ago if you hadn't insisted on keeping the dress a secret from me until now."

"I wanted to make sure I fit into it and could afford it before I showed you." She stepped off the platform and went behind the curtain of the dressing room. "You're still free for lunch, right? There's this amazing café a few blocks from here."

"Lead the way, lady."

Ivy saw how long the line was and stepped up to the male employee at the podium. "Hi, table for two?"

He stared at her for a moment, and said, "It's a twenty-minute wait, miss. Please wait outside."

"It's my friend's wedding tomorrow." A white lie never hurt anyone. She gestured to Fawn, which seemed to be the magic key because he grabbed two menus and said, "Right this way."

When they sat down, Fawn fixed her with a knowing look. "Okay, fess up. What's bothering you?"

"I don't want to bug you. You're getting married in two days and the last thing you need to do is worry about your maid of honor. It's supposed to be the other way around."

"Come on, Ivy. I'm your best friend. And it'll only stress me out more if I know that something's bothering you."

Ivy was grateful when their waitress came over to their table, poured their water, and asked for their drink orders.

"I'd like a glass of rosé, please," Fawn said.

"Me, too," she said. Ivy picked up the menu and hoped Fawn would let the subject drop. Unfortunately, she found what she wanted within two seconds and her best friend knew her well enough to know that she would only be stalling if she kept the menu in front of her face.

Fawn raised an expectant eyebrow and Ivy sighed. "Alec is worrying me. I know he's hiding something from me."

Her friend didn't say anything and took a sip of her water.

"What should I do?"

"Well, you could just talk to him."

"I can't."

"Why not?"

"Anytime I want to bring it up..." she trailed off. "I can't ask him. I don't think I want to hear his answer."

Fawn leaned forward. "I think you should take your own advice and ask him about it. That's what you told me when I first met Caleb and look how that turned out."

"True." She saw her friend smile and added, "Do you know what's going on with him? He's not going to break up with me, is he?"

"Why on earth are you even thinking that? Of course, not. Alec is a lot of things, but he's not indirect about *anything*."

It was true, but that didn't make her anxiety go away. If anything, it made it worse.

Their wine arrived, and Ivy took a large sip. "Tell me what you need from me for the next twenty-four hours. You already nixed my bachelorette party idea, so what do you want to do?"

"*That's* because Caleb and I promised not to have those parties. Besides, neither of us wanted one." Her friend pointed at her. "Just relax, Ivy. I don't need you to build a new itinerary on short notice. That would make me a real bridezilla."

"You could never be like those nightmare brides."

"Let's order, I'm starving." Fawn waved the waitress over. She rattled off her order, and Ivy did the same. When she was gone, Fawn said, "You know what you could do for me?"

"Anything."

"Let's have a sleepover. I feel like we haven't had one in forever."

"That's because we haven't. What with you living with Caleb. You never want to go out anymore."

"Can you blame me? And it's not like I'm the only one. You've been with my brother." She paused. "It's still a bit weird saying that, but I'm still so glad it's you."

Ivy suppressed her smile. It was true, though how long that was going to last now worried her.

"No," Fawn said. "You're not allowed to worry about that anymore. Sleepover tonight until my wedding. I'll tell Caleb to stay with Alec."

"Well, I need to go home to pack, but then we could go out to the movies or..." she saw Fawn's inner introvert emerge and smiled. "We'll just watch them on the TV. Did you ever get around to watching that remake? I know you were looking forward to it."

"No. I kept meaning to, but life got busy. And besides, Caleb didn't want to see it. He doesn't get why everything needs to be redone."

"He has a point."

"He's being a pain in the ass. I love him, but sometimes his being alive for so long is a real killjoy."

"You sound like me."

"I blame that on spending too much time with you."

Ivy raised her glass. "You're welcome." They both took a sip. "So, movie, sleepover, I'm assuming strawberry ice cream for you and chocolate for me. Wine, red or white? Why am I even asking? Red, obviously. Caramel Ghirardelli squares. Anything else?"

"Your pajamas, normal stuff, clothes for the next few days, and of course, yourself. It's going to be fun."

A LEC HEARD THE DOOR OPEN AND SHOVED THE small velvet box at the bottom of his sock drawer.

"Alec?"

"In here," he called. She came into the room, her eyes dropping to the bed where he'd placed her partially packed suitcase.

"Are you trying to get rid of me?"

Yes. "My sister called. Heard you were having a sleepover. Tried to pack as much as I knew you'd need. But since it's her wedding and you're the maid of honor, I'm sure there'll be more you need to add."

A strange expression crossed her face before she smiled at him. "That was thoughtful. Are you sure you'll be okay with Caleb staying here?"

"Yeah. We're good now." Since the angel had proposed to his sister, they'd come to an understanding. He clearly loved Fawn and had more than proven himself.

"You've never hung out alone," she pointed out as she pulled out a clothing bag from the closet and laid it into the suitcase. He watched Ivy continue crossing the room over and over as she packed.

"True... but I'm sure we'll find something to talk about."

Twenty minutes and two bags later, Ivy was fully packed. He walked her to their apartment door. He gave her a peck on the lips. "Have fun."

She wrapped her arms around his neck and lengthened the kiss.

He grabbed her waist and pulled her into him. Eventually, she pressed her hands against his chest and he let her go.

"Don't get into too much trouble when I'm gone."

He smiled. "I could say the same to you."

"Me?" she feigned innocence. "We're just staying inside and having a sleepover."

"Like you haven't done crazy stuff on sleepovers before. If you remember, I was there for most of your stupid pranks."

"They're only stupid in your eyes because you fell for so many of them. Don't take it personally, it was just so much fun."

He bit her earlobe lightly. "Don't corrupt my sister anymore before her wedding. I'll see you soon."

She laughed. "See you soon." She kissed him one more time and hit the elevator button. He waited until she was inside, and the door closed before he went back into their apartment.

A LEC STOOD UP AND CLEARED HIS THROAT. NEXT to him, the newlyweds and Ivy smiled at him. He addressed the crowd of their closest family and friends who filled the large hotel ballroom. The ceremony had been much smaller, but even now, the guest list was shorter than a lot of their other friends' weddings. He saw Caleb's ghostly family but knew that their human friends definitely couldn't. It was still somewhat funny to see his normal and magical worlds so close to each other.

"Hello everyone. You all know me as Fawn's older brother."

"*Twin*," his sister corrected just like he knew she would, earning a round of laughter from the audience.

He pointed at her. "Those seven minutes count, sis. And since you gave me only seven minutes to make this speech as revenge for that fact, I'll move on. Being a twin isn't easy. People assume you're super similar, they like dressing you up in matching *everything*, and they also make constant jokes about knowing what the other is feeling, like every group of twins has the powers of Luke and Leia."

His sister smiled.

"I've since come to the conclusion that being compared to those two isn't that bad. And not that far off. Because while we sometimes drive each other nuts, we love each other and will always be there for one another. And I can now happily say that you have another person who will be there for you no matter what."

He took a short sip of his champagne and placed it back down on the silk purple table cloth. "Anyway, it's not exactly a secret I wasn't an immediate fan of Caleb, here. But can you blame me?" He heard some murmurs in the audience, no doubt wondering and worrying where he was taking this speech. "This super handsome guy swept my sister off her feet and I wasn't there to give my brotherly stamp of approval. It didn't matter anyway. There was no way I could change my sister's opinion of this man. And I can understand why. He has proved that he will go to the end of the world for her. And your love for each other has inspired me to find it in my own life."

He reached out his hand, willing Ivy to take it. She did hesitantly, and he led her in front of the long wedding party table. Her expression clearly screamed, *what are you doing?* He maintained eye contact with her, silently telling her to trust him, as he slowly got down on one knee in front of her and everyone else.

She stared at him, her hands flying from his grip and up to cover her mouth.

He reached into his pocket and opened the black velvet box holding his grandmother's engagement ring. "Ivy Moore, will you make me as happy as the newlyweds here and marry me?"

She didn't respond for a moment. And in that moment, his heart beat the fastest it ever had. Fighting Lucifer's army seemed like a soak in a spa hot tub in comparison to this.

"Yes! Alec—"

He rose up and cut her off with a kiss. He heard the guests "aw" and applaud, but he didn't care. The room could have been empty for all he cared. In that moment, he bet he was even happier than his sister, the bride, on her own wedding day. Because the woman he loved, his soulmate, had just agreed to make him the happiest man alive.

I VY HELD ALEC'S FACE AS THEIR TONGUES ENTWINED. When they finally broke apart, she sent a sheepish smile to Fawn. She saw Alec lift the microphone to his mouth again.

"I'd apologize for that, but I'd be pretending that I feel any regret. And, I had the bride's permission, so, I'll quickly finish this best man's speech, so everyone can start eating."

Ivy took that as her cue to sit back down. Fawn grabbed her hand under the table and gave it a squeeze as she sat down.

Alec turned to his sister. "As your brother, I've always tried to look out for you. And though you called me overbearing at times, I've only ever wanted the very best for you. So, tonight, I congratulate you for starting this exciting new chapter in your life." He raised his glass to her. "Cheers to the bride and groom."

Ivy heard everyone repeat his words, then silence as everyone took a sip. "I've taken enough of everybody's time now, so the last thing I'll say is have fun tonight. I know all of us up here will."

He sat down next to Caleb and sent Ivy a heat-filled look which had her blushing.

"Save it for the dance floor," Fawn whispered.

"Oh, shut up," Ivy whispered back, smiling and practically salivating at the fancy salad that was placed in front of her. She ate quickly, even while talking with Fawn, Caleb, Alec, and Stella. "Are you excited for your honeymoon?" she asked.

"Yes," her best friend said. "But my *husband* won't tell me where we're going."

"I want to surprise you," Caleb said. "Where did it say in our marriage vows that that was no longer allowed?"

"You know I don't like surprises. Can't you just tell me? I promise I'll be happy anyway."

"Just remember," Alec piped up, "you signed up for a lifetime of this when you decided to marry my sister."

Caleb merely smiled. "That, I did."

EPILOGUE

THREE YEARS LATER

Alec's phone rang. *Shit*, he'd forgotten to put it on silent before they went to bed. Although, that wasn't really surprising given how fast they'd fallen into it. He reached over Ivy's still sleeping body and held it to his ear. "Hello?"

"Alec? Hey, did I wake you up?"

He rubbed his eyes. "No, no, I'm up."

Ivy turned over and mouthed, "Who is it?"

"Dylan. Go back to sleep," he silently answered. He got out of bed and said into the phone, "What's up with you?"

"I wish I could say it was smooth sailing, but I actually have a favor to ask you."

Alec suppressed a yawn. "Sure, what is it?"

"There's a coven of witches in New Orleans that's posing a bit of a problem for my pack." His friend cleared his throat. "They cursed my soulmate a while back—"

"Wait, your soulmate?" Fawn had told him that Dylan's had died before he found her.

"Long story. Anyway, would you be able to come down here to... I don't know, convince them to be nice? My dad and I have tried every bargaining trick we can think of and they just won't lift the curse."

"Um, my mom might be better equipped to handle the situation."

"Yeah... between you and me, my dad and your mom had an argument a few weeks ago, so I don't know if that's a good idea."

Alec blew out a breath. He *did* know. He'd been in the same room with his mom when the phone call happened. It was bad, to say the least. "I mean, I can definitely come down, but I'll need more info. How soon do you need me down there?"

"By tomorrow, if possible? I'm sorry it's so last minute. I thought I could handle it, but my soulmate may have pissed them off further. Who knows what would happen next? I don't want to find out."

"I can *definitely* understand that." He glanced back at his bedroom where Ivy had no doubt fallen back asleep. "Speaking of soulmates, can I bring Ivy?"

"Of course, you can. But you might want to tell her that there's not a lot of parties for us werewolves in the Quarter since this whole thing with the witches started."

He smiled. "I'll be sure to pass that on. See you soon."

"Thanks, Alec. You're a life-saver."

"No problem, man." He ended the call and went back into his bedroom. He was surprised to find Ivy was already dressed and brushing her hair in the bathroom. "You're up."

She sent him a smile over her shoulder. "Of course, I am. You weren't exactly quiet on your phone call. Besides, even though I don't have a magic link to your mind like Fawn, I could feel your anxiety through the wall. What's up? What did Dylan want?"

Alec walked to his closet and pulled out his suitcase. "He wants me to go to New Orleans today. Want to come with me?"

"Well—I'd have to pack."

"Great. He didn't say how long we'd be there, so maybe pack for a week?"

"Okay, but Alec, why are we going?"

"Some witches in the Quarter hexed his soulmate and he needs me to negotiate with them."

"Soulmate?"

"Yeah," Alec kissed Ivy on the lips then searched for a lock he could use. He always seemed to be losing them. "He said he'd explain when we got there."

He heard her mumble, "he better," and smiled.

I VY SQUINTED, EVEN BEHIND HER EXPENSIVE SUNGLASSES, THE Louisiana sun was painfully bright.

She turned and saw Alec hauling both of their suitcases behind him. She had offered to help him, but he had waved her on. She followed the crowd until she saw Dylan standing next to a giant pick-up truck.

He saw her, too, and opened his arms. She gave him a hug but pulled back quickly. "Ugh, you're sweaty."

"It's summer, city princess. Get used to it out here."

She stuck her tongue out at him and looked around. "So, where is this soulmate of yours anyway?"

"She's back at the house. You'll meet her soon enough, but don't scare her off."

"If she's worth it, she won't be intimidated by me. Just please tell me it's not Bailey."

Dylan smiled. "No, it's not. But you may see her since she's still in the Pack."

"Ugh, don't remind me."

Alec finally came up and wrapped his arms around her waist from behind. "Hey, man. Mind helping me get these in the truck?"

"No problem." Dylan grabbed both suitcases, waved his foot under the bumper, and lifted their luggage into the compartment with ease. He shut the trunk and hugged Alec. "Thanks for coming."

"No problem."

Alec opened the passenger door and helped her into the seat before climbing in behind her into the surprisingly spacious back seat.

"Nice leg room," he noted.

Dylan didn't even cast a look back as he buckled himself into the driver's seat. "It has to be. Werewolves aren't exactly small."

"No, kidding," she said. She was still shocked at how strong he was.

They drove for two hours, during which time Ivy napped in and out as they went through the city and made their way to the swamp.

Dylan rolled to a stop outside a wooden house large enough to be a small hotel. "Welcome to the home of the Morsure Pack."

OTHER BOOKS

THE BELGRAVE LEGACY

SHORT STORY COLLECTION

TAMING THE ALPHA

ACKNOWLEDGMENTS

First and foremost, I would like to thank my friends, family, and most importantly my *readers* for supporting my writing. Thanks to them, I have learned that needing help is never a sign of weakness.

Shout out to Jennifer Munswami (JM Rising Horse Creations), your artwork always leaves me speechless. Thank you for making my book look stunning.

Important note: authors live on reviews. And so, I ask you, my wonderful reader, to leave a review on your favorite retailer, and recommend this book to your friends.

I'm already working on the third and final novel in this trilogy, *Taming the Alpha*, Dylan's love story. If you want to be kept in the loop about all my future publishing endeavors, subscribe now at zarahoffman.com/subscribe, and you'll receive the first three chapters of the final book.

ABOUT THE AUTHOR

Zara Hoffman is a college student and has been writing since she was eight years old. She spends most of her time doing homework and writing new stories because if she didn't, her head would likely explode. Her books are for young adults or the young at heart. After all, growing up is overrated.

www.zarahoffman.com
zarahoffman@zarahoffman.com